ORIGINALS RIDE

Hellions Motorcycle Club

CHELSEA CAMARON

D1519615

ORIGINALS RIDE

A Hellions Ride

HELL RAISERS DEMANDING EXTREME CHAOS

USA TODAY BESTSELLING AUTHOR
Chelsea Camaron

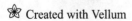 Created with Vellum

ORIGINALS RIDE
Hellions Ride: Book 8

The Hellions were born from danger and chaos. It's time to take it back to where it all began.

Four men, four families, four originals, one club.

Go back to the first ride for Roundman, Danza, Frisco, and the late Rocky Fowler. From brotherhood to growing their own families, they have always had each other's backs.

A life choice, a road less traveled, all coming together in the name of brotherhood.

Some found love, some faced loss, and others learned real loyalty. This is the story before the chaos.

This is how the originals ride.

Series Reading Order:
One Ride

DEDICATION

To my dad, Roundman, you are the man who stands behind me through everything. You taught me to love unconditionally, ride hard, be myself, and not to take one person for granted. You are always who you are and make no apologies for it. Thank you for being the man who rode the Harley before it was the cool thing to do. You are a badass rebel with a heart of gold. Thank you for being my dad and always being solid in my life.

To my mom, you are the original "ol' lady." You've been my strength when I've been weak and my safety net as I spread my wings to fly. Thank you for being the strong woman you are.

To Haywood and Rocky, you were taken all too soon. Haywood, I can close my eyes and still see your smile and the way your eyes lit up when you always said, "Let's give 'em something to talk about." I know my dad misses you more than words, as we all do. Until the time comes when we can ride together again, you are in our hearts. Rocky, I sure miss you stopping by the shop to check in. They do a ride in your honor for charity. It brings back every memory, and to see all those bikes from so many clubs and organizations that wouldn't otherwise come together line up and ride together is a moment of pride for you and everything you stood for. The two of you were a class above the rest, men who stood up for everything they believed in. Thank you for the friendship you gave my dad and everyone who knew you both. Thank you for being an extended family and solid people to look up to.

To all the Hellions' readers, the series is coming to a close with *Originals Ride* and *Final Ride*. Thank you for encouraging me and loving these boys as much as I do. We only have a couple of rides left together, and I truly hope you feel the emotion and the family bond I wrote the books to have. For me, writing an MC was never about the grit, the violence, the shock, and awe; it was about the feel of the ride and the power of a club family. I'm fortunate enough to have people in my life who aren't my blood but are my family and have my back through the good and bad. My wish for everyone is to experience the unconditional love that comes from a bond that's solid, whether it's in an MC or a reading book club, people coming together to lift each other up, be a positive force in someone's life so we don't have to travel through life's miles alone.

LETTER FROM CHELSEA

Dear Reader,

While the Hellions Ride books have each been written to stand alone, they are best read in order. This book will go between the past and the present and clear up almost everything that has purposely been left out of the previous books. It will be told from Roundman's point of view mostly with an occasional part from the other originals. The opening of *Originals Ride* is before the Hellions came to be, so please understand they are not a club at the beginning of the book.

To have the best reading experience, here is the series order:

One Ride

Forever Ride

Merciless Ride

Eternal Ride

Innocent Ride

Simple Ride

Heated Ride

Ride With Me (*Hellions MC* and *Ravage MC* Duel)

written with Ryan Michele

Originals Ride

Final Ride will be the final book in the Hellions Ride

series releasing late 2016!

Thank you for taking a ride with the Hellions MC.

PART ONE

PART ONE INTRODUCTION

Sometimes, the family we choose for ourselves can be more loyal than those we are connected to by blood. Ride until I die, the Hellions Motorcycle Club is my family.

~Roundman~

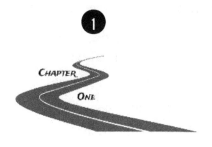

CHAPTER ONE

EYE ON THE PRIZE

ROUNDMAN

"Dia, why're you with a dirty man like me?" I look at the blonde-haired, blue-eyed beauty in front of me with her high-cut jeans flaring out at the bottom and her tube top doing nothing to hide the points of her hard nipples. Her hair fans out from her face like she's an angel in a magazine.

She taps her finger on her chin as if she's thinking about it. "Rough fingertips over smooth skin ..." She licks her lips as I reach out and grab her hips.

"Bad," I growl, leaning down to bite the curve of

her neck. "Winding me up while I'm at work. Brick house, baby. You're a brick house."

"Sugar, you asked the question." She bats her eyelashes innocently. "I just answered."

Without any shame, I slap my grease-covered hands over the globes of her ass and squeeze. "I'll give you rough fingers, baby."

"Don't tease me; just please me." She leans up and presses her lips to mine. Like every time we touch, the sparks roll through me as if I have fire burning in my veins.

"How the hell did I get so lucky? I'm from the wrong side of the tracks. You're all class, sass, and goodness … I'm just a working man."

"Who's not afraid to get a little dirty," she chimes in with a flirtatious smile.

"You with me just to make your daddy mad?" I ask, pushing her when I already know the answer.

"I can do a lot of things to tick off dear old dad, Blaine. I don't have to be with you for that."

"Love you."

"Good to know," she says, pulling out of my grip. "Whatcha gonna do about it?"

"We're gonna go there again?"

She moves beyond the front counter of the garage I work at to the office space. She wants more, and I damn sure will give it to her, but not until I get life in order. First, I have to get my shit worked out so I'm not busting my knuckles for an hourly paycheck. Clive's been good to me, but there are areas Tommy, my best friend and coworker, and I see the potential to grow the business. Clive is old school and doesn't want to risk branching out. One day, though, it's going to be ours—mine and Dia's.

Before either of us can continue the conversation, in strolls her chump of an ex, Paul Watson, her high-rolling high school boyfriend, entering like he owns the damn place.

Well, clue in, fucker. I'm going to own it. In time, this garage will be mine, just like Claudia is already mine.

"Claudia, Claudia, still wasting your time pining away over this cat. When are you gonna let me have another chance?"

"You followin' me, Paul?" Dia asks bluntly with a hand on her hip and agitation showing.

"Baby, you're not that good. I'm here to see Clive with a business proposition."

My gut churns, and anger boils inside me like a volcano about to erupt. How dare this punk come in here and think he's going to give Clive a business proposition. I have busted my ass in this shop since I was thirteen years old. I earned my place. There's no way in hell Paul or anyone associated with him will come in here to take it away from me.

I don't have much in life, but my dad always told me a man's work will speak louder than his words; a man's drive will take him further than riding alongside someone else; and sometimes, a man waits because, when the perfect opportunity presents itself, a real man will be ready ... and in position to make a play.

My work speaks louder than my words, and my drive has gotten me this far and will only take me further. I will be damned if I do it on someone else's coattails, dime, or plan. The opportunity is here; the time is now.

"Clive ain't got time to listen to any proposition from you."

With a smirk of arrogance that makes me want to punch his teeth in, Paul steps back with his hands in the air. "He ain't gotta listen to me. Just give him a message. My uncle and his brothers are riding in next week, and they wanna talk one on one."

Stepping out from behind the front counter, I stand toe to toe, towering over Paul. "Last I checked, I'm a mechanic, not a messenger boy." With a sneer, I look down at him. "Looks like that's all you."

He steps back, trying to put space between us, and I feel Dia stand at my back but not moving to pull me away. It makes me proud that she takes her place, but I'm on edge that she even has to do it in the first place.

"Give him the message, Blaine. I promise you, if you don't, the next message I'll be giving to my uncle will put your name on a radar you don't want to be on."

"Your uncle ain't shit, Paul, just like you. The town talks. He beat the hell out of his woman and took off to Florida. Ain't nobody seen him in years and not a damn person in Haywood's Landing has missed him, either."

"Watch yourself, Reklinger." He looks around my hulking frame at Dia. "Claudia, when shit goes down, that's the last man you wanna align yourself with."

Two soft hands grip my forearm as I feel her heat come closer. "Paul, there are a lot of people I shouldn't align myself with, but the one I trust with everything is Blaine, so I've got his back until the day I die. You should learn a thing or two about loyalty like that."

He shakes his head. "I cheated. I fucked up, but I'm tellin' you, Reklinger is gonna start himself some trouble he can't work his way out of. Don't wanna see some fine piece like you go down with him."

"You threatenin' me?" I say, gritting my teeth and clenching my fists to contain the rage inside.

"Nope, just trying to make sure my message is clear. Let Clive know who's comin', or you're gonna be the one who pays the price, not me."

"I'll fuckin' kill you with my bare hands before I do any biddin' for you or the likes of you."

"Suit yourself." He turns and walks away, leaving me cosmically pissed the hell off.

"Blaine," her soft voice calls to me. I turn, and my eyes meet her blazing blue ones. "Don't let him shake you."

"I'm nobody's messenger."

"Never said you were, baby. Just don't let him cost you even one minute of getting off track." A devious smile plays on her pink lips. "How'd you say it?" She deepens her voice and contorts her face into a serious look, mocking mine from the other night. "Got a plan, Dia. Gonna get Clive to let me buy the shop then gonna buy the lot next door and build us a house. Gonna marry you and make you round with my babies all the damn time. Gotta work, darlin', but mark my words, Claudia Moakler, you're gonna be my wife, and this is our forever. I'll bust my ass, my knuckles, and my knees to make your every dream come true."

With grease-covered fingers, I tip her chin up. "Glad to know we're on the same page." I press my lips to hers as she wraps her arms around my waist and melts against me.

She pulls away slightly. "Keep your eye on the prize, Blaine." Each word causes her lips to brush against mine.

Moving my hands down to cup her ass, I scoop her up as she wraps her arms around my neck and legs around my waist.

"How 'bout I keep my *hands* on the prize?"

She laughs as I carry her back to the stock room. She won't be laughing long as I promise to make her mine for a lifetime while I make her moan my name in the moment. If only every day at work could be about me pistoning in and out of her pussy instead of lubing the pistons of a car.

Rocky

"Goin' cruisin' tonight; you wanna ride?" I ask over the fence that has separated our two houses my entire life.

"Daddy says you're trouble, Tommy. Don't know if he'd want me in a car with the little hellion next door," Marie answers shyly, and I just laugh. "He says you've given your parents hell since the day you came screaming into the world. Mom thinks you have a rebellious streak bigger than the whole town."

"Maybe I was born to give your daddy hell when I take out his girl. As for bein' a rebel, well, bein' good sure don't get me nearly as far as forging my own way, Marie. That's just the plain truth."

"Who says I'm gonna go out with you?" she challenges, but the hitch in her voice gives away her interest.

"One ride, baby. You know you wanna hear how that Camaro rumbles from the inside."

"Show off," she replies, but it's not a no.

"Gotta go to work. I'll pick ya up at nine, Marie. Be ready."

On a happy sigh, she says, "Okay, Tommy, I'll see ya tonight."

I make my way to my car with a smile.

Marie has grown up as the girl next door. From her pigtails that she got gum in once so her mom had to cut all her hair off to the woman with large breasts, a skinny waist, and toned legs, she is a prize. Her dad should be worried about her taking a ride with a boy like me.

The things I want to do to her … Just thinking about it gets my dick hard. First, though, I have to get through work. The house I just bought doesn't pay for itself. In fact, I came to my parents this morning to get the last of my things. Marie was out in her front yard, looking delicious in her strapless romper. I had to give it a shot.

I'm not looking for anything serious, but a cruise down to El's Drive-In would be fun. Then maybe I'll be able to give her a tour of my new place, get her opinion on my new bedroom—that sort of thing. I laugh to myself as I get in my car.

Clive's shop where Blaine and I work is a short drive down the road. He's been my best friend since we got in a fight in elementary school. The little chump cut in front of me in line. I shoved him into the wall; he shoved me back. At eight years old, we were rolling around the hall, trying to get hits in. We both got three paddles and a phone call home. The next day, we were the best of friends and have been inseparable since.

Look, when a boy gets his ass beat in front of another boy and you both refuse to shed a tear no matter how hard the hits were, you bond. That's Blaine and me. No matter how hard the hits come at us, we take them together.

For life, I'll be by his side, and he'll be by mine. No matter whom we have sex with, whom we break up with, and whom we one day settle down with, Blaine and I will face it together.

DANZA

"I'm hitting the road, Mary Alice," I yell from the kitchen to my girl in our bedroom.

I hear her scurry out, and then she is rushing up to me. Her strawberry blonde hair is puffy on one side and flat on the other from how she was sleeping. She's in my T-shirt, which hangs down to her knees. There's nothing more sexy than my girl waking up satisfied by me and covered by my clothes.

She wraps her arms around my neck and crashes her lips to mine. Knowing she has nothing on under the shirt, I slide my hand up her inner thighs.

"Gonna miss you," she whispers breathlessly against my lips.

"Gonna miss you," I say, giving her bare ass a

squeeze before sliding my fingers through to dip inside her.

"Rhett," she moans, rocking into my hand. "You're gonna hit the road late if you don't stop."

"Just giving you something to think about while I'm gone, sweet thang."

"You ain't right," she gives me back with a smile before she kisses me again.

Scooping her up, I wrap her legs around my waist as I let her ass rest against the countertop. "Gotta have you one more time."

After unzipping my jeans to free my hard cock, I slide inside her as she bites her bottom lip.

"Love you, Rhett."

"Mary Alice, you were made for me." I move in and out of her as she tightens around me.

She drops her head to my neck, sucking hard. No doubt, she's leaving her mark. It only turns me on more as I slam inside her harder and faster.

"Mine," she growls, and it sends me over the edge, spilling deep inside her.

Mary Alice and I have been together forever. The way she wants me drives me to do better, be better, and give her the world. I'm the poor boy from the trailer park whose mom was a whore to get by. She's the woman from the perfect family behind the white picket fence, and somehow, she fell in love with me.

I barely made it through high school. I beat the shit out of everyone who looked at me wrong. In fact, when we were ten, that's how I met Blaine and Tommy. Blaine gave me a stare, and I swung out, only to miss and have Tommy take me down football player style. Blaine pulled him off me. It was two on one, and I wouldn't back down. Yet, they stopped themselves from beating the shit out of me and, instead, asked me to play kickball after school. We've been raising hell together ever since.

Mary Alice and I got together, and for the first time in my life, I had a family of my own making. Tommy and Blaine are like my brothers. Hell, I practically lived at their houses, spending the night at one or the other's based on whose parents would let me stay. Mary Alice would pack me a lunch with her own for school to make sure I ate something good.

When school started to get hard, Mary Alice pushed me to stay in. The hours that girl spent helping me with homework and studying for tests ... I promised her, when we graduated, I'd give her a house and provide for us. The only way I could do that was to learn to drive a truck. Over the road, they call it. Well, it pays the bills so my girl can have it easy, but it leaves little time for us to be together.

I won't say it doesn't get lonely sometimes, taking me back to the feelings I had before Tommy, Blaine, and Mary Alice came into my life. It is what it is, though, and we all get by together. We make it work.

With one last kiss to Mary Alice, I leave her with my come dripping down her legs before I zip up my pants and head out. I'll make a quick stop at Clive's to have Tommy and Blaine keep an eye on things for Mary Alice, and then I'm westward bound.

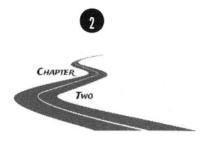

FURY

ROUNDMAN

Two weeks go by, and things are smooth. Dia and I found a little trailer on the beach to rent. Her parents didn't approve of our decision to live together before getting married, so they made her leave everything behind. No problem. She's mine, and I take care of what's mine.

Besides, my parents gave us the sleeper sofa they had for a few years for our bedroom. It's not the most comfortable bed in the world, but with Dia beside me, it sure feels like I'm sleeping on a cloud. Then a client came in with an old Ford Pinto that needed some work. Rather than wait for the car to get fixed, he sold it to me cheap. My buddy Tommy helped me in our down time to get her tuned up. So now my girl has a ride that I can trust, a job she may not love, but she likes—waiting tables and making pies at the local pizza shop—and a place of our own.

If I keep working hard, I'll get her a ring. Then I will make an offer to Clive on the shop, and we will have it all.

Tommy and I are out back, tossing tires into the tree line, when a rumble catches our attention. More specifically, the distinct tick of a group of Harley Davidson motorcycles. Tommy and I both ride. I have a Sportster, while he has a Duo-Glide, both from the early sixties but both solid bikes.

Haywood's Landing is a small town in North Carolina off highway 58 near the coast. There's not much to the area and especially not too many that ride motorcycles.

One, two, three, four … The bikes keep piling in, finally stopping at eight. I'm not the kind of man who rattles easily, so the number of men doesn't intimidate me, though it should.

After tossing the last two tires into the woods, Tommy and I make our way back to the shop, thinking Clive would be taking on a big job with all these bikes pulling in. We are one of the only shops in the area that work on motorcycles, and although an unauthorized dealer, we do carry the name brand parts and accessories from time to time. We are happy to have any opportunity to show Clive where we can do more.

This is where Tommy and I see expansion. Clive wants to stick with cars. I want a shop for bikes. Tommy, he sees the potential with bikes, but he wants to restore the classics as well as modify the cars of today to be faster. I swear the man should go work for Winston Cup Racing, but he likes coastal life, and that would require him to move.

Walking in through the back, we are too comfortable.

When I hear Clive's raised voice, I barely pull myself back from storming right in unprepared.

"Ain't doin' shit that has to do with no gangs. Fury, Fuckery—I don't care what you call yourselves —you got no place in my shop." He sets the strangers straight as I battle my instincts to rush in.

"Watch yourself, Clive," a gruff voice says calmly, too calmly. "We're a brotherhood. I get we're in small-town Carolina, but we're a motorcycle club. We are an organization, and we want to do business with you. We aren't here to take anything from you, but rather work with you. However, if we have to take, well"—I hear the guy give a half-chuckle—"we will." There is a pause before the man says, "By any means necessary."

My blood runs cold, and roaring fills my ears. Instinctively, I grab the small Beretta Tomcat pistol off the shelf in the stock room where dust covers every inch of space since we don't often clean. There are seven rounds in the magazine. I double check the gun. One thing about Clive, he likes handguns to always be loaded and in reach. He always told us, *"Ain't been robbed and ain't about to get robbed."* Well, I'm not about to let Clive down. He has been clear that he doesn't want to do business with these men, whoever they are, and it's time they see their way on down the road.

When I open the door and enter the office area, my heart stops. A man stands in front of Clive, not more than ten feet from him, with a gun aimed right at his chest. There are six other men all dressed in jeans, leather, and motorcycle vests, standing around with stone cold faces. I don't see the eighth man and assume he's out front as a lookout. I don't have enough rounds in this gun to take them all out.

"This don't concern you two boys. Go on," the

man wielding the weapon says, waving us away with the barrel of the gun.

I look at Tommy, who moves closer to the desk where we both know there is a revolver just under the top.

If I have to use this, I better make every shot count then pray like hell Tommy can cover the other men.

"You two deaf or dumb?" another man in the back with a beard that goes down to his belly roars. "Go on and get!"

"Ain't leavin' Clive," I say, deepening my voice and steeling my spine.

"Loyalty," the man with the gun says. "I can admire that. See, Clive? You got yourself some good ol' boys here who understand loyalty. This will do you right good for our business."

Clive clenches and unclenches his fists. "I said no."

"Thought Cheeks said the old man would be easy to work with?" some guy in the back with his front teeth missing hollers.

"Don't you worry about it. Cheeks' nephew made contact for us. Clive here will cooperate."

Nephew ... Uncle? Then it hits me.

Fucking Paul Watson! As soon as I get Clive out

of this mess, I'm going to beat the shit out of him.

Tommy has moved into position behind the desk to easily grab the revolver. With the counter top for both of us to use for cover, we are in the best spots we can be. Clive, however, is not.

I mentally start sorting out the proximity and ages of the men. This all calculates into their reaction times. Based on Tommy's location to mine, he has a blind spot to two of them, so I need to hit the main guy then those two in rapid succession.

Each shot has to count. There will be no second chances today.

The man with the gun looks at me. "If Clive can't be reasonable, I'm sure one of these young men will understand that business is business, and our deal is a lucrative one."

I look at Tommy who nods at me before he scans the men again, most likely doing his own mental calculations since his rounds are limited, as well.

"Clive has a good business goin', fellas," I try to reason. "We appreciate you stoppin' in and all, but you know what they say, '*If it ain't broke, don't fix it.*' Clive likes things how they are; it ain't my place or yours to change that."

The man smiles at me with a wicked grin. There is no remorse to be seen, no empathy—nothing. The man in front of me is a dead man on the inside, and if this keeps on, I'm going to make sure he's dead on the outside, as well.

"Blaine, Tommy, go on out back and finish those tires. We're closing up shop for the day," Clive instructs then steps back. I can tell he's trying to get to the front counter where he can have cover and possibly reach the desk.

"We're good," I reassure him. "Tires are done. We'll help see your guests out and lock up," I stand my ground firmly. I don't care if I die today. I will do it, not backing down to these assholes. Fear doesn't hit me; adrenaline keeps me at the ready. I have the love of a good woman, and I'm going home to her tonight, dammit.

The man raises his gun and slides off the safety as he aims for Clive's head, stopping him from reaching the safe zone behind the counter. "Think you should reconsider, Clive. You only get one answer."

Without giving the man an opportunity, I pull the small Beretta from behind my back and fire.

One shot.

One bullet to the head.

I don't wait. There is no time to hesitate. I have to make each and every second count.

I take out the other two who pose a threat to

Tommy as he fires shots at the others. They have no cover as Clive moves behind the counter, and we continue to take the men out.

Four are down solid. Dead.

Dad always told me it's not the size of the gun that matters, but where the shot lands. Thank anything that's good left in this world today that he was right and he taught me about weapons. I'm grateful for all those times he took me hunting or just out shooting as I make all my shots count.

One man takes a shot to the thigh from Tommy, and he drags himself toward the front door. Clive fires the kill shot, and blood splatters on the walls of the entryway.

The man from the outside turns and looks inside. Before Clive, Tommy, or I can get a lock on him, he's running off. The next noise we hear is the sound of his bike starting up and riding off.

When the men all cease to move and the blood covers the floor, I look at Tommy then Clive. There is a fresh scrape to Clive's neck where a bullet grazed him from one of the bikers, but he's breathing and still with us, so that's all that matters.

"Damn, Blaine." Clive shrugs his shoulders, no doubt feeling the weight of what just happened. "One round, one man. You are a fine shot, son." His eyes go to Tommy. "You did good. I can't imagine what would have happened if you two hadn't been here to back me up."

Pride fills me, but then I look at the carnage in front of us again. I wait for the remorse. I wait for the guilt. I wait for the shame. Only, it doesn't come.

Instead, I only find relief that, after this is done, I get to go home to my woman and still have a job with my boss man breathing to come back to. I don't know what these men came here for. Honestly, I don't care. Clive said no, and they felt using force would gain them their request.

Well, they thought wrong.

Clive's been good to me and doesn't deserve one bit of this. I'll take his back any day as if he were my own dad. Those men picked the wrong place to try to force their agenda.

Paul Watson better watch out. If the police don't lock his ass up when they finish here, I'm going to find him. And when I do, I'm going to beat him so badly his own mother won't recognize him.

He will know he need not mess with what's mine. Fury MC should know, after today, they need not ride into my place, looking to force any deals. No one messes with what matters to me. This shop, Clive, Dia—hell, the whole damn town—it's all mine.

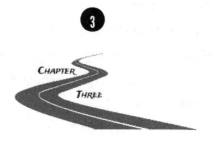

ENDLESS POSSIBILITIES

ROUNDMAN

"We're gonna have to take you boys downtown to get your statements," an officer says with his hands on his stick and the butt of his gun as if we pose some threat.

Looking around at the bodies on the floor, I shake my head. The shock is setting in. Taking a life—a man's life—even when threatened, weighs heavily on my soul. This isn't like shooting a deer to have meat. In the moment, however, I couldn't think. I had to eliminate the problem.

Now it hits me, though.

I lean over and dry heave as I fight back my need to vomit everywhere.

Clive claps me on the back. "It's okay, son."

Standing up, I ready myself to go in with the cops as the paramedics take out one man at a time in black bags on their gurney.

Moving to the desk, I pick up the receiver on the telephone. My fingers shake as I try to focus on turning the numbers on the rotary dial.

"Zella's Pizza," Dia answers.

"Dia, it's me."

"Blaine, you orderin' lunch, baby?"

"No. Something happened today. If Paul comes by there, you stay away from him. After work, you go to Mary Alice's until I come pick you up."

"Time to go," the cop says to me, and I hate that I can't explain to her what's going on.

"Blaine, you're scaring me." I can hear the worry in her voice.

"Nothing to worry about. Just don't be alone and don't go anywhere near the chump. Clive, Tommy, and me gotta ride to the station."

"Beaufort, you're going to Beaufort, not Cape Carteret," the officer informs me while still giving me the space to talk to my girl. I can respect him for that, even if he looks like he's ready to jump out of his skin from dealing with me.

"Why are you going to the jailhouse?" Dia asks bluntly.

"I didn't do anything wrong. Some of Paul's—"

"Time's up," the officer says.

"Look, I promise I'll explain everything later. Just promise me no talking to Watson and you'll go to Mary Alice's."

"I promise, but if you need me to come bail you out, I'll be there."

"I hope not. Love you, Dia."

"I love you, Blaine. Whatever is going on, we'll get through this."

With her reassurance, I feel some of the weight lift off me. No matter what anyone says, I wouldn't change a thing today. Clive was in danger, and I won't ever turn my back on him when he's always had mine. The only thing I would change is I would have kicked Paul Watson's ass the day he came in, playing messenger boy.

After hanging up the receiver, I head out the front door, unable to avoid stepping in blood. Promptly, the fresh air hits my nostrils, causing me to hunch over and dry heave more.

"You two get in the back of my patrol car. Clive,

we expect you to follow us in your truck."

"Understood," Clive says to the officer. Then to Tommy and me, he says, "Boys, it's all right."

Is it really? Is anything ever going to be all right again? Who were the men we just killed? Did they have families? I know they were bad men, but why were they here?

All the questions dance in my mind as I climb into the back of the Plymouth Enforcer beside Tommy. I want to laugh stupidly at the fact that Clive gets to drive himself in, but Tommy and I have to ride in the cruiser. Funny how everyone always says we're hell raisers, yet today, we were simply trying to have a good man's back.

The ride is a blur as I keep trying to figure out why the men were at Clive's shop in the first place. His business has always been on the up and up, so why would Paul Watson put him on anyone's radar?

I still have no answers when we pull up to the Beaufort courthouse and police station. Our local office is small and more of a hub for the west side of Carteret.

Immediately, they separate the three of us into different rooms. I'm in a small office with a table, two chairs, and nothing else.

A different officer comes in and takes a seat

across from me with a file in his hand.

"Not your first time here, Mr. Reklinger."

I drop my head. This man can't be serious right now.

"Did some dumb shit a few years ago. Joyride was all it was."

He opens the folder to pull out a blank piece of paper. Sliding it to me, he unclips a pen from his shirt pocket and tosses it on the table in front of me. "I'm State Bureau of Investigations Agent Westlake. We need your statement of today's events in writing."

"Okay," I agree. There is no point in arguing. As much as killing is wrong, what other choice was there? I couldn't let them hurt Clive, and I'm certain they would have killed us all if we didn't bend to their will or shoot first.

Leaning over the table, I begin to put into words what happened this afternoon. When I finish, I lay the pen over the paper. I look at the man across from me who has remained emotionless.

"Do you have any questions for me, Mr. Reklinger?"

"No," I answer, knowing better than to ask a cop anything. My words won't get twisted. He has my statement in writing, so now I just need him to let me go.

"Well, I have some for you."

I nod my head but don't speak. I don't have money for an attorney, and I don't see how I would need one. But in the end, this is my situation in the right here, right now.

"Did you know the men you shot today?"

I look the agent in his eyes, having nothing to hide. "No."

"You have no affiliation with any members of Fury Motorcycle Club out of Central Florida?

Fury motorcycle club, hmmm. Why does Paul have an uncle in a gang coming to Clive's shop? my mind questions, but I simply answer the man in front of me with, "No."

"Why were the members of the outlaw gang at the shop today?"

"Look, I don't know anything about a motorcycle club, outlaw gang, or those men today. Tommy and I were slinging tires out back when we heard 'em pull up. Came in from the back, saw Clive was in trouble, handled it."

"Shoot first and ask questions later?"

"No, watch the man's back who has always had yours," I bite back at him.

"Did you know Fury MC were here to proposition Clive to run guns through his parts shipments?"

"No. Why would you tell me something like that?" I ask, wondering if I'm getting set up. Small town politics leave me trusting no one.

The man doesn't answer, only stares at me.

"Look, Paul Watson came in the shop the other day. He said he had a message for Clive that his uncle was coming to see him. That's the only warning we had that *anyone* was coming."

"Paul Watson, you say?"

"Yes," I say through clenched teeth as my aggravation grows. How dare this man sit here and think I would set Clive up? How do I know this man isn't tied to Fury himself? The longer I sit in this room with this man who gives me very little information, the more questions I have.

He scribbles on the folder then rises from his chair. When he opens the door, I think he's going to leave me in here, but he turns to me.

"You're free to go, Mr. Reklinger."

I'm standing to leave when he holds the file up in the air.

"Just don't go far," he says with a snicker as he turns his back on me and walks out.

I just killed a group of men who tried to bully my boss into something. One shot in each and he wants to get smart with me? I don't know if I want to clap him on the back and say thanks for letting me go or get pissed that he acts like there is more going on here. I didn't know a single one of those motherfuckers who came in today.

I hate cops like him. They think they are above everyone because they carry a gun and a badge. Well, Clive ain't never done shit to anyone, and where the hell were the boys in blue when he needed protection? Sitting at a desk somewhere, eating a damn donut, that's where!

As I make my way down the hall, I look to see if I can find Clive or Tommy. Not seeing either of them, I head outside to find them both waiting for me in front of the building.

"What the hell they do to you back there?"

I shake my head. "Just questions."

Clive wraps his arms around me in a hug. The old man trembles against me. "Thank you, son. There ain't shit to worry about. The cop told me it's all self-defense. Thank you, Blaine." He pulls away, and I can see the tears in his eyes threatening to spill over. "Ain't never been scared a day in my life. Swear to the good Lord above, if it was my time to go, I'd go, but not without a fight. Thank you, both of you"—he looks from me to Tommy—"because without y'all boys, I wouldn't be going home to my wife tonight."

Tommy looks at me then Clive. "You gave us a place to work and stay outta trouble." He kicks the rocks under his boots. "Well, you gave us something to put our mind to so we weren't gettin' into trouble. We can't let nothing happen to you, old man." With a smile, he tries to lighten the mood between us. "You know them guys?"

Clive shakes his head. "All I know is they call themselves Fury MC. Something about being outlaws from Florida. They wanted to use my lot as a drop point, transporting stuff from Florida to New England. I don't have a clue what they were runnin', but I don't want nothing on my property that ain't mine."

Transporting. What the hell could some outlaw biker gang from Florida possibly want to transport from one end of the country to the other? And the State Bureau of Investigations is involved. My mind runs over everything. The agent said they want to run guns. Transporting guns through old Clive's shop seems ridiculous, though. The more I think about the different things they could push for later or in the long run, the more my head hurts.

The truth is scary. The truth is that the possibilities are endless.

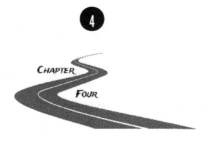

CHAPTER

FOUR

PLANS CHANGE

ROUNDMAN

C live drops us off at the shop where Tommy and I left our bikes. With nothing more than a wave good-bye, I climb on old faithful, my Harley Davidson Sportster, and speed off.

Rhett and Mary Alice live on a three-acre place surrounded by corn fields. High school sweethearts, they moved in together right after graduation. If it weren't for Mary Alice, I doubt Rhett would have finished school. He drives a truck, and thank fuck he was in town today when I sent Dia over there. He's in and out of the area so much sometimes he can be gone for a few hours and other times, it's for days.

Mary Alice is a tough broad and wouldn't let anyone get to her girl, but I like the comfort of knowing Rhett is home, too. He's gone more days than he's home, so I got lucky he was in town. Mary Alice could handle herself if need be—Dia, too—but I feel better knowing my friend has my woman's back. With their house out in the open, no one can approach without them knowing it first.

Rhett is on the front porch, lighting up a smoke, as I pop the kickstand down.

"Damn, Blaine, Dia said you went downtown."

I nod as I step up beside him.

He pulls his pack of cigarettes back out to offer me one.

"Nah, I'm good. Just need my girl."

"Wanna tell me what happened so I know what you set on my doorstep first?"

"If I had answers, I'd give 'em to ya. I just needed to know she was safe while I was unavailable." I run my hands through my long hair, retying it back in a ponytail down my back. "These fellas rode up on Clive today."

"So I heard. Small town talk and all that."

"Shit!" I feel panic like a punch to the gut. "What does Dia know?"

"You and Tommy took out seven members of Fury MC, a group of outlaw bikers from Florida. According to the local news, you're, like, a damn hero, man."

I drop my head. "A hero, I am not."

"To the girl inside my house, you are."

Just as I get ready to answer, the front door flies open.

"Okay, Blaine Reklinger, I gave you time to walk in that door and sweep me off my feet, but you take too damn long, so get over here and kiss me."

I can't help smiling at the way her blonde hair flies wildly around her face and how her hand is perched on her hip while she wears her black work shorts and red top. She taps her foot impatiently.

When I don't make a move, she springs forward, jumping onto me and causing me to step back, almost sending us both off the porch. She wraps her arms fiercely around my neck as her legs come around my waist, and she holds on tightly before planting her lips to mine. I open, inviting her in, and she devours me as our tongues collide and teeth clank. I can't get enough.

Breathlessly, she pulls away from my lips, but not

my body. It's then I can see the puffiness in her face, the redness in all her features, and the evidence of tears shed. My heart breaks. I never want to cause this woman pain.

"You're alive," she whispers, closing her eyes and resting her forehead against mine. "You're with me, Blaine, really here." I can feel the relief wash through her as her body relaxes, and I take her weight. "I love you more than the moon, the stars, the sun. My God, Blaine Reklinger, I love you," she whispers with her lips brushing against mine with every word.

"Claudia Moakley, I was only afraid of one thing today." I pause, pulling my head back so she will open her eyes to see mine. "I feared I wouldn't have this moment right here. Baby, I know we have a plan, but I can't." With a squeeze to her ass, I say, "No, I won't waste another minute by waiting to have life in order. I wanna marry you, Dia. You, me, ride for life, that's it. I promise you the ring, the church, my name, and whatever you want, but baby, right now, I gotta know it's me and you together forever."

She smiles brightly and presses her lips to mine. "Always yours, Blaine."

I hear Mary Alice squeal excitedly as I deepen the kiss with my woman, my future wife, and I do so with the knowledge I could have lost it all today.

Without untangling herself from around me, Dia pulls back and looks at her best friend. "Looks like we have a weddin' to plan." She turns her head back toward me, her eyes dancing in happiness. "And soon."

"Whatever you want, baby." I kiss her again.

Refusing to release her, I look over her shoulder at Rhett and Mary Alice. "I'll be in touch, man. Gonna take my girl home now."

Dia laughs against me as I turn around and carry her to my motorcycle. When I climb on and get it started, she hops on right behind me. The minute her hands wind around my waist, something changes inside me.

Every plan I had changed today and every single one of them for the better, but right now, this feeling I have for Dia is far deeper and more encompassing than anything we have ever shared before.

We hit the open road of highway 58, and the roar of the engine calms my mind.

Dia roams her hands under my T-shirt, finding her way to the skin of my abdomen and causing my muscles to flex involuntarily. The sensation of her legs against mine, her chest pressed to my back, and her hands around me makes it feel like she's a part of me. Like the bike under me, she's an appendage of my soul. The wind whips around us, and her hair flies around us both, hitting me in the face and reminding me I'm alive.

I am alive, and my woman is with me. We are one.

I twist the throttle, the bike spits oil like it always does, and Dia laughs against me as she tucks her head into my neck. I feel her lips first then her teeth as she nips, her legs tightening against mine. She runs her hands up my chest before she slowly traces down my waist to my jeans where she squeezes my cock through the denim.

I am alive, and my woman wants me. We are one.

Pushing the bike harder, I'm careful as we ride not to hit a bump yet still pressing the vibration through us both as I turn onto highway 24 rather than make my way to our place on the beach. When the turn for Nine Mile Road comes up, I slow without coming to a stop; instead, I roll us onto the road.

Nine miles of open road, nine miles of tight curves on a narrow road with the woman I love. Nine miles of life remembered. Nine miles of life cherished. Nine miles of a life of new beginning.

Nine miles, I ride. Me, Dia, and nothing but pavement beneath us. Then, when I can't fight the need to be inside her anymore, I take my woman home and make love to her, knowing that plans change, life kicks us in the ass, but one thing that will never in my lifetime change is the love I have for the woman with me.

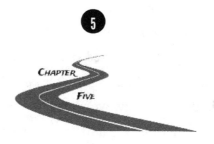

CHAPTER FIVE

DREAMS

ROUNDMAN

C live told Tommy and me to take a few days off. He even offered to pay us to do it. In good faith, I couldn't let the man clean up the mess on his own, though. Therefore, Tommy and I both arrive at the shop on time as if it were any other day on the calendar.

Only, it isn't.

We both look like hell and heaven all twisted into one. Knowing what we came so close to losing yesterday, it's obvious Tommy slept about as well as I did, which was none. The glimmer in his eyes and the way his woman Marie drove by here on her way to work just to blow him a kiss tells me they had a similar night to Dia and me. They haven't been together long. What started out as a hookup may be turning into something more substantial. Only time will tell, and yesterday, we almost lost it all. We both had the weight of taking a life on our shoulders, but at the same time, we both know, if we hadn't, we wouldn't be here to experience today at all.

We don't make it in the front door before the sound of a single Harley pulls up. Instinctively, Clive comes to the door, and we turn to see who it is.

Rhett twists the throttle, causing the bike to rev before he rolls into the parking lot.

"Figured you could use an extra hand," he says, climbing off the steel machine.

"It's appreciated," I tell him as two then three cars pull in.

We stand in awe as more people arrive, all to lend a hand in the cleanup of the front office for Clive.

When I look over at the man who is as much a father to me as my own dad was, I see tears in his eyes. The events have shaken him. The age and worry stand out in his features unlike before.

The day moves quickly as each person takes on

task after task. When the afternoon comes to a close, the front looks brand new with the fresh paint on the walls and new seats donated from a local dentist office. Even the shop is spit shined, and we got rid of some of the old oil stains. The town really banned together today in the wake of a tragedy.

As everyone says their good-byes, Tommy and I are profusely thanked for stepping in to save Clive, and finally, we are left with just the three of us.

"Boys," Clive says as we stand behind him while he locks the front door, "did some thinking last night. Talked it over with the missus, and we made a decision."

"Don't think now is the best time to be making decisions, Clive," I say suddenly, worrying over what the future holds for my job. I have more than me to think about. Claudia can't go home since her parents have made it more than clear, if she's with me, she's not with them. I have to provide for us. Clive can't close the shop because of Fury. If so, they win, and they cannot win.

"I'm no spring chicken. The time has come to find out if retirement really means you get tired." He lifts the keys to the front door. "Blaine, you've been here every day since you were barely a teen. There ain't an inch of this property that your hands haven't worked on." He takes my hand in his and turns it palm up. The cold metal of the front door keys hits my skin.

I shake my head in shock. My mind goes back to the day I almost lost it all.

The blue lights come on behind us. I should pull over. I should stop the car right now. I should do the right thing. Only, Tommy and I aren't exactly the registered owners of the car we are currently riding in. In fact, if Clive finds out we're taking this particular car out on a test ride, I'm sure he would have a heart attack.

The Plymouth belongs to Mr. Johnson who is a personal friend of some big wig in racing. The engine compartment no longer houses the stock engine but a larger Chrysler engine, instead. Everything is in line with the MOPAR family to make this a real contender to hit the track if that is the client's intention.

Tommy and I didn't bother to learn anything about the car. We simply took the first opportunity we had to take her out for a spin. Only, we had to wait for Clive to get off work and go home, which left us to take this beast out at night.

Small town, quiet roads with a loud, fast race car ... Well, we should have known we would get caught.

It wasn't long before the cop had the car parked on the side of the road and Tommy and me on our way downtown. He calls Clive who comes and picks us up at midnight.

"I should have left you two in there. A night behind bars, sleeping on a hard rack, might get through to your hard heads."

"Clive," I start to explain as we get to his old truck.

He throws his hand up to silence me. "You boys have so much potential. Don't do stupid stuff that takes away from that. Gotta remember business is what keeps ya going for the fun stuff like racing your own car. Working ain't about the fun stuff; it's providing for it, boys. Don't confuse the two."

Without another word, Clive drives us home. Knowing we disappointed him upsets me; his quiet burns deep.

"Don't fire us, Clive," Tommy says barely above a whisper.

"Fire you? If Mr. Johnson wants to, he can practically shut my business down with this stunt you two pulled."

"Shit," I mutter.

"Fifteen-year-old boys and you think you know everything. If you would have wrecked that car, who would have paid to replace it? Huh, boys? Was your fun worth costing me everything?"

"No, sir," Tommy says, hanging his head in shame.

"Integrity, boys. What you do when no one else is watching is what really makes you a man. Supporting the people who have taken a chance on you and not taking advantage of them makes a real man. So you tell me, what should I do with you?"

Clive could have beaten our asses, fired us, and even more, he could have marched into our houses and told our parents. He did none of it. Instead, he left us to have the integrity to tell our parents ourselves. When we both showed up for work the next day, he made sure we cleaned up the Plymouth and did all the work on it after hours at no charge. We also had to tell Mr. Johnson ourselves what we did and give him free service for life from Tommy and me. To this day, ten years later, I'm still changing the man's oil regularly and not getting a dime.

Clive could have sent Tommy and me away. He should have turned his back on the two young boys who made a mess of his business more times than I care to admit, but he didn't. Somehow, he's here, giving it all to us.

"The time has come, son," Clive explains. "Do right by your customers; do right by your partner, Tommy here. The shop, the land, the business, it's all yours. The lawyer's drawing up the papers. Tommy, you get a thirty percent lifetime ownership so Blaine can't do anything fully without you." A lone tear falls down his face. "Man's gotta know when he's not in the best shape to keep on keepin' on. Yesterday, they got the best of me. I'm slipping. Age is catching up to me. I went in blind to them and had not one damn thing on my side but God and you boys. That's all the warning I need to let go."

"Are you …? Are you …?" I can't seem to get the words out as I choke on so many emotions. "Are you really sure? We can leave things alone, Clive. You take some time off then come back."

"Never been more sure of anything, Blaine. I'm leaving it in good hands."

CALIFORNIA KID

ROUNDMAN

Tommy and I talked. Until Clive gave us paperwork, and honestly, even after, we would treat things as business as usual. We didn't save him to push him out of his shop. We did it because it was the right thing to do. Never leave a good man to struggle alone.

The sound of a Harley pulling in not long after we opened the next morning causes Tommy and I both to go straight outside. After everyone came together to clean up the last mess, no way are we risking anything going down like that again.

Hopefully, the boys from Fury MC aren't stupid enough to come back here. If they are, Tommy and I both have our revolvers ready. The SBI kept the weapons from the other day, but we had more, so we aren't empty-handed.

Behind the bike rolls in Rhett in his rig. Without shutting it off, Rhett jumps out of the truck and heads over to the man on the Harley. They shake hands, and then Rhett points over to Tommy and me before the guy even dismounts.

We make our way over to see a man with black hair slicked back and a goatee. He's in a black T-shirt, faded jeans, and boots. Just like Tommy and me, a chain hangs on his side from his belt loop to his back pocket holding his wallet. The chain isn't a statement like people think. It's there so that, if our wallet slides up and out of our back pocket while we ride down the highway, we don't lose it. The man's saddlebags show wear; the bike obviously has some miles under it. Good to know.

Rhett lifts his head to us. "Blaine, Tommy, this is the California kid, Richard Billings."

Richard extends his hand for us to shake.

"Met him on the road back in Bama. Told him, if

he made his way to Coastal Carolina, this was the best place to get his bike serviced."

"Thanks, man," I say to Rhett who often meets people on the road and tells them, if they are ever in the area, to stop here for work. Rarely do we ever see them.

"Need a new rear tire and oil change," Richard says.

"You affiliated with Fury?" Tommy asks with an edge to his voice.

"Fury MC, as in the gang from Florida?"

"Well, I don't know. You tell me; how many Fury MC's are there?" I give back, not liking that he's avoiding the question.

"Look, man, these fellas had a run-in with some boys from Fury. Can't be too safe," Rhett explains to Richard then looks at us. "Richard here is from San Fran. He's got no affiliation. He rides where the road takes him." Rhett pauses. "Alone."

Only then do I extend my hand and shake Richard's. "Welcome to Haywood's Landing, Frisco."

We all laugh as Richard raises his hands in the air, questioning the nickname.

"Richard makes me think of Dick, and the only dick I wanna think about is the one in my pants as I'm in my woman," I explain.

"Amen, brother." Tommy backs me up. "Well, Frisco, pull her in bay one, and we'll get started to get you back on the road."

"Got a local haul. I'll be back by this afternoon, guys. Frisco, stay for dinner; Mary Alice is making roast. I hate leftovers, so you'd be doing me a solid by eating. Y'all come, too, if you want. I'm sure Mary Alice would love to have Dia over." He looks at Tommy with a smirk. "If you're gonna make a go of things with Marie, then bring her on over, too. You know the girls gotta give their stamp of approval. Better sooner than later, Tommy."

Two hours later, we have two new tires on and have given Frisco's bike a solid service. Good thing the man doesn't mind getting his hands dirty, because Tommy had to work on a Bel Air for a regular client, so it left me on the bike.

Taking a break for lunch, we are all sitting on flipped over buckets in the bay area. Tommy lights up while I open my lunch from Dia and take a bite of my sandwich.

"How long ago was the situation with Fury?" Frisco asks, and Tommy takes a deep drag off his smoke.

"What's it matter? They came. They were handled."

Frisco raises his hands in surrender. "Nothin', man. Not tryin' to upset you, Rocky."

Tommy raises an eyebrow at him.

Frisco smiles with the whitest teeth standing out against the dark hair of his goatee. "Things are obviously rocky with us. Just trying to lighten it up, man." Frisco looks at me. "Look, I get your reasons not to trust. I'm not with Fury, or any club for that matter. I've done a lot of traveling, seen a lot of clubs like Fury. Not all of them are about the bad stuff. Some are just a brotherhood of men takin' each other's backs."

"Really?" Tommy asks in a tone that seems hopeful.

"From what I've seen, this won't be the last you hear of Fury. They'll be back. You gotta ask yourselves if you're ready for that."

"Shit," I say, putting my sandwich down, having suddenly lost my appetite.

"They're looking to move stuff through here. They aren't going to simply ask once and move on. I've seen this in plenty of small towns. You're off the radar, easy to get stuff passed through by car or by boat."

I didn't think about any of that. He's right, though. This probably isn't the end of Fury MC.

I look at Tommy and see the same thoughts are going through his head.

"Well, Rocky," I begin, "what the hell are we gonna do to keep our town safe?"

He laughs at my calling him by Frisco's nickname. "Well, brother, reckon we better have our own thing going on so we are more than a two-man show when they roll back in. Gotta show them ain't no one coming to Haywood's Landing to cause mayhem. No, any hell raisin' going on here is controlled by us."

The three of us laugh. The situation is daunting, but we have to make light of it after everything that has happened, or we may just drown under the pressure. Together, we will keep Fury and men like them out of our town.

Picking my sandwich back up, I feel okay again. "Yup, we control the chaos."

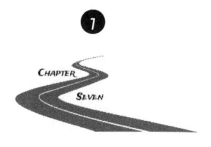

CHAPTER SEVEN

HELLIONS RIDE

ROUNDMAN

One week later, Frisco, the California kid, is still in town. He spends his days helping at the shop and having dinner over at Rhett's before crashing on his couch.

Rocky and I are at the shop when four bikers pull up. The leather vests are all too familiar with the blue Fury flames and patches covering each one of them. Despite different sizes, different rides, and different sayings, each vest—or cut as they call it—is unique.

With a tire iron in my hand, I step in front of the

shop. The revolver at my back feels too far away, but I know Frisco and Rocky are inside, armed, and on their way to back me up.

"Whoa, whoa, whoa, boy," the first man to climb off his bike says, raising his hands high in the air. "Ain't here for that kinda trouble, young buck."

Young buck, huh? I'm twenty-six years old, and in the last week, thanks to his club, I feel like I have aged well beyond a rational number.

The other three men climb off their motorcycles, all with their hands raised. Good thing, too, because I'm in no mood for round fucking two.

The men approach just as Frisco and Rocky flank me on either side with guns held high. The sound of a diesel engine approaching causes us all to pause.

I fight back a laugh as Rhett comes hauling ass into the parking lot with his big rig. He turns at just the right moment to avoid hitting the bikes but blocking them in. As he locks the brakes and slides to a stop, dust flies around the chrome and leather, settling onto it.

The tension in the air is thick, and I watch the men closely as they see Rhett climb out of his truck with his shotgun in hand.

"Got shit to do, fellas, so you can find your way out of town," I say to the group of men.

"Just came to talk business. I've heard the shop has new owners. Well, we have a proposition for you," the man tries.

I stand my ground. "Ain't got time to listen to a damn thing any of you has to say."

"I think you fail to realize who is in control here," he starts, and I raise the tire iron to shut him up.

"I think you fail to realize where the hell you are. I'm no young buck. I'm a one shot, one kill, it only takes one round kinda man. You have two seconds to turn your asses around and head back to the shithole you came from before I put each of your names on a bullet and make sure to take you out with that single shot each. This is our town, and we don't want none of the likes of you around here."

"Just think about it for a minute, son—"

"I'm not your son," I growl.

"If we don't do business through you, we'll do it with someone else in town. Why don't you be the one to make the profit?"

"You are a crazy son of a bitch," Frisco says as the man clearly doesn't want to give up.

"Take highway 24 on your way out and get back to the interstate or hit highway 58 to 17," Rhett informs as he tosses his rifle to me, and I catch it right after I drop the tire iron. He doesn't know about the revolver at my back, and now isn't the time to tell him. "Either way you go don't matter; it's just your time to go."

The man in the back with a beard down to his belly turns to Rhett, dropping his hands. "Who the hell are you?"

"The man giving you directions on how to get the hell home."

He moves to stand toe to toe with Rhett. "We ain't done talkin' to the young buck yet."

The man twists as if he's reaching for something, and Rhett reacts, hitting him with a right hook to the jaw. Instantly, the man is knocked out.

His buddy jumps into Rhett's space, nailing him with a good one to the face and causing his nose to bleed. Rhett doesn't hesitate in giving the guy a jab to the gut then an uppercut, making him stumble into his friends.

Rhett then brings his hands up in a boxer's stance, ready to keep going. Man number two throws his hands up in defeat, and man number one groans, coming to.

"As you can see here," I say to the largest man who has been in front of me the whole time, "we like how we have things now. Unless you want me to use the two bullets I got in this shotgun—one for you and one for your buddy beside ya—I suggest you get on your way."

"One round, one man, huh?"

Irritation is reaching the point of becoming anger. "I'd say ask your brothers, but seeing as how they each took one shot and aren't around anymore to tell ya about it, I reckon actions speak for themselves."

"Fury could use men like you," he states calmly and honestly.

I shake my head at him. "Not interested in your way of coming into people's towns and trying to force them into your world."

The man laughs in my face, only making me grip the shotgun more tightly and wish he would give me a reason to blow his head off.

"Brotherhood of your own making, huh?"

"Yeah, we're the Haywood's Landing Hellions, and this is our town."

The two men Rhett fought back away from our group as they tap their brothers on the shoulders.

"Send Watson to handle this. We have somewhere to be," the bearded chump informs. "And locals are looking for us. Let's go."

"Yeah, you got places to be, so go on so we can get back to work," Rocky says, dismissing them.

"This won't be the last you see of us. We know how to find you, Reklinger."

The fact that he knows my name pisses me off. "Well, I would hope so since I'm in the same place you found us before. Ain't leavin'."

The men back away, never turning their backs on us as Rocky, Frisco, Rhett, and I stand in our places at the ready if they decide to pull something.

Anger rushes through me. How dare anyone think they can come to my town and control what goes on in my business?

Their vibrations of their pipes echo off Rhett's rig as they make the tight three-point turn to get out.

Frisco is the first to move. He gives Rhett a playful shove to the shoulder. "Damn, Danza's got moves."

"Huh?" Rhett questions, looking at us for answers.

"He doesn't get to watch much television. He doesn't know about the guy on the TV show driving a taxi who is also a boxer," Rocky explains.

"Does he have good hair?" Rhett asks as he pretends to style his back.

"Oh, definitely just like you, Danza," I give him a hard time. "Moves and great hair. The ladies are just lining up."

"Okay, Roundman, 'I'm gonna put your name on a bullet.'"

We all laugh, but then the weight of the situation settles on each of us.

"Fury isn't going away easily," Rocky is the first to state.

"Then I guess they'll have to learn this is how the Hellions ride," I say with all the confidence in the world.

Frisco looks at each of us. "Well, I haven't stayed in one place this long in years. Looks like I might just have to dig myself some roots." He smiles with his white teeth shining brightly. "Danza, that couch of yours has been nice, but you think Mary Alice could find me a place of my own?"

"You serious?" Rhett asks happily.

"Way I see it, I've spent enough time on the road, and Fury ain't going away. If I'm gonna take a stand for something, I'll stand for the Hellions in Haywood's Landing, then."

We all nod, agreeing. Frisco fits in with our group of hell raisers. He may not be a local, but he stood with us today like he is one.

For the first time since Fury rode in on Clive, things finally feel right again.

Yes, Haywood's Landing is our town. Anyone

who wants to come here and try to control it will learn all about the Hellions.

Today, the Haywood's Landing Hellions have been born. It comes out of necessity, but the bond between us is still one of brotherhood, and together, we will stand strong against anyone who chooses to cross us.

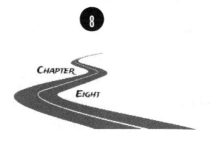

CONTROL THE CHAOS

ROUNDMAN

Two months go by, and Paul Watson has been out of town the entire time. Quiet, things are too quiet. Rocky, Danza, Frisco, and I don't believe it.

In the meantime, the Hellions have formed. We don't ride alone, and together, we are determined to keep Fury out of our town.

In all of Frisco's travels, the man made connections, the kind that gave Danza the idea of changing his business runs. With his office inside ours, we get to stay close and monitor what is moving through Haywood's Landing. With Frisco now at his back, Danza is no longer on the road alone, which Mary Alice appreciates.

Business has been good for Rocky and me. He's expanded to doing some custom rods and restoration projects that involve fabrication and not regular mechanics. I've been able to get a few more bikes rolling through, which is what I prefer to do. Add in the clients Clive has had for years, and we are making this work.

Little by little, the four of us have found our way of controlling the chaos that crashed into our small town. Still, I want a piece of Paul Watson. His day is coming.

Lying in bed on a lazy Sunday with Dia's naked body draped over mine—nothing tops this. Absolutely nothing. I trace my middle fingertip up her spine and back down all the way through the crack of her plump ass. She moans groggily against me. My morning wood only gets harder at the feel of her scissoring her legs over me.

"Gonna marry me today?" I ask, to which she kisses my chest before her blue eyes meet mine. "Gonna go to bed tonight as Claudia Reklinger?"

"Every night from tonight until the day I die, Blaine, I'm going to be Mrs. Reklinger."

I smile at her. "Has a nice ring to it." I massage her ass with my left hand while I tweak her nipple with my right.

She slides the sheet off both of us and moves to straddle me. When she sits straight up, her nipples poke out in the air as my erection stands up against the crack of her ass, wanting in her heat.

I lean over to the nightstand and pull out the small box I tucked away in there yesterday. "Got you a gift."

She bites her bottom lip as I set the small box on my chest then move my hand down to her golden curls between her legs. Pushing my thumb between her lips, I stroke her, applying a bit of pressure to her bud so I can feel her juices mix in my pubic hair and skin. She rocks against my thumb, getting us both wet with her arousal.

"Gonna open it or you gonna ride my hand?" I ask as I feel my dick pulse with need to be in her.

"Both," she says in a heady whisper as she keeps her rhythm and lifts the box.

Shifting my hand, I have two fingers sliding through her lips as she continues to grind against them.

I watch the smile on her face grow as she looks into the box.

"Mary Alice said you hated the something blue tradition. She said y'all went everywhere, looking for sapphires earrings so blue they looked black."

She stops her hips and nods.

"Took a run with Danza yesterday. Stopped off in Raleigh at the big store and found these. You gonna wear 'em when you become my wife?"

Carefully, she moves the box containing the earrings to the table. Her tits are in my face as she does so, and I take full advantage, putting one in my mouth as I play with the other. She laughs and moans as the sensations hit her.

Without speaking, she moves back, causing me to sit up as to not lose her nipple my tongue currently circles.

She strokes my dick as she positions it at her opening then slides down, taking me all the way to the hilt. The feel of her muscles gripping me has me releasing my mouth and throwing my head back in ecstasy.

"Blaine Reklinger, how did I get so lucky? Got a man who takes my back. Got a man who provides, protects, and keeps his promises. Got a man who goes out of his way to give me good. Sugar, your woman is gonna give you good now." A devilish smile plays on her plump lips as she slides up then rolls her hips on the way down my shaft as her walls contract around me.

She moves her hands high up in her hair as her tits bounce freely. She rides me and doesn't hold anything back.

"Love you, Dia," I groan out as I hold back my own orgasm.

Her rhythm becomes erratic as she sends herself over the top, and then I finally thrust up and release deep inside her.

"Gonna be my wife tonight."

"Can't wait!" she says, collapsing over me with my dick still inside her.

We are one. Ride until we die.

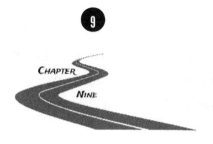

THE FUTURE LOOKS BRIGHT

ROUNDMAN

ONE YEAR LATER

Who would have thought a year ago that Rocky and I would not only have our own shop, but be in a situation to divide the business into two separate ones?

Rocky had a wild night with his childhood friend who grew up literally next door. Marie and he have been steady for a while since their hookup. Most recently, the results of their premarital activities have

Marie swollen with their first baby. A quick wedding tied up any loose ends for any of the Bible slinging biddies around here.

It took Danza a little while longer to get his head out of his ass and make things right with Mary Alice. A small beach ceremony much like the one Dia and I had made her Mrs. Rhett Perchton, all while wearing my woman's earrings.

Women and those wedding traditions … I don't need to understand them. Whatever makes Dia happy keeps me happy, end of story to me and the men I know.

The Haywood's Landing Hellions have grown. We had a few men prospect for us and patch in. We are an organized group with bylaws and a real system for both the shop businesses and the transports Danza and Frisco are running.

We keep things tight. No man is ever alone.

To make things official, we decide to take a ride to Deals Gap, NC. There is a buzz going around about a ride known as "The Dragon." It's a challenging course of mountainside and tight curves that carries you into Tennessee, all lining up on a map to look like the shape of a dragon's tail.

With Marie home with little Dina, the four of us make the trip, leaving the other members behind to help her out until we make it back. Rocky and Frisco ride solo, and Mary Alice and Claudia proudly take their places behind Danza and me.

The ride there is rough in some places, only making Dia hold on more securely. Just how I like it. We stop at the Deals Gap shack to pull over and stretch our legs. Then, before we get back on the road, I pull Dia to me.

She's in skin tight jeans and a black tank top with a jean vest. Her blonde hair is back in a braid that I wrap my hand around then pull her head back to look up at me.

"Love you, Dia."

She smiles brightly at me. "Love you, Blaine."

"Love having you on the back of my bike," I tell her, rubbing the whiskers of my goatee against her jawline.

"No place I'd rather be," she whispers before I press my lips to hers in a kiss that is sloppy and loud, and I don't give a shit who watches.

The four of us then climb on our rides, starting them up before Mary Alice and Dia settle in behind Danza and me. I raise my left hand high in the air, throw a finger forward, and then we take off.

Danza rides to my right as my VP. Frisco is behind me as our enforcer with Rocky riding beside him, taking up the rear as our sergeant-at-arms. We make the eleven-mile ride through over three hundred curves in the same line up with Dia's arms holding me tightly.

Brotherhood, family, love, life, and the open road —this is what living, really living, is about.

As we finish crossing over into Tennessee, we pull over. I look at each of my Hellions brothers one at a time, and silently, we all agree this is the final patching ride for every member in the future. This is the ride that will make men out of boys on bikes. With one wrong move, not only would you hurt yourself, but your brother would go down, too. This is a ride to bond. This is a ride about life, loyalty, and love. This is our ride for now and forever.

Fury MC has stayed away. Paul Watson moved to Florida, and we haven't heard a thing from him or his uncle's group. That doesn't mean we let our guard down.

There are more clubs out there than the men of Fury, and Haywood's Landing is a good place to use as a go-through.

We should know.

Not only are we getting our own piece of the transports, but we have a little spot out in the Croatan forest where we have a little Mary Jane business growing. A little bud ain't going to hurt anyone. The government just wants to control it. Well, they get enough tax money, and I won't be giving them any more.

The risks are high, but the rewards are there. We have built this from the ground up, and we are making it work, not only for ourselves but our town.

PART TWO INTRODUCTION

PART TWO

PAST

OUT OF LOVE & LOYALTY...
IT CONTINUES

"When it all falls apart around you, whoever is still with you will be with you always. Trust, believe, and give your all to those who don't walk away when the going gets tough. Life is always going to test you. It's how you overcome your failures, your losses, and how you face the next day that defines you."

~Roundman~

CHAPTER TEN

ASS AND SASS

DANZA

The double-wide in the middle of a field is my little piece of heaven. The woman inside is an angel and a true gift. My job is unpredictable and keeps me gone more than I'm home. With grace and strength, Mary Alice holds down the home fires while I chase a dollar down the highway.

She's a good woman. The best.

She's also all I know. We've been together since forever, and even though I was slow to make an honest woman out of her, she's mine, and she's my wife.

She's also pregnant. Very pregnant. And my sweet, calm Mary Alice disappeared the same day she found out, it seems. Rocky says it's the hormones, and once she has the baby, things will go back to the way they were. According to him, I need to take the high road and understand everything I do is wrong. This is not easy for a man like me, which is probably why I feel the way I do right this moment.

I'm sitting in the front yard on my Harley, wondering what tonight will bring before I walk inside.

Last night, I epically fucked up. When Mary Alice asked me to take her to the Dairy Queen for a hot dog, I should have done it. Instead, I let the pregnant woman waddle her way out to her Chevrolet Corvair, get in, and drive off in search of her hot dog.

Only, the car broke down, leaving a very pregnant Mary Alice on the side of the road in the July heat, waiting for someone to come along to help her.

I suppose, when it had been over an hour, I should have gotten up and gone to look for her. After all, we normally don't let anyone in our group travel alone. It's just all these crazy cravings and mood swings are too much for me to handle. The more she changes, the more I find ways to stay away.

I've been an ass. I don't deserve her, yet she's still inside the house we share, waiting on me.

Getting off my bike, I open the saddlebag and get the bundle of flowers I stopped off for then make my way inside.

The smell of food cooking hits me as soon as I step inside.

"Mary Alice," I call out, taking off my boots at the front door.

No reply.

I don't find Mary Alice in the kitchen or living room. When I head to the baby's room, I don't see anything out of place, and I also don't see my wife.

Peeking my head into the guest room, still no sign of Mary.

"Mary Alice!" I yell as I make my way to our bedroom, to which I get no reply.

The bathroom door is closed, but that doesn't stop me since she won't answer.

I hear her crying as I turn the knob to find the door is locked. Adding force, I easily break the knob to enter just as she jumps and turns around.

Before I can speak to find out what's wrong, she turns back to face the toilet, leans over, and hurls.

Dropping the flowers in my hand, I quickly move to stand behind her and hold her hair back.

"Baby, I'm sorry. What can I do?" I ask as she heaves and I try to rub circles on her shoulders with my free hand.

"Cut your dick off," she says as she continues to vomit.

My balls automatically draw up at the thought.

"Dinner smells delicious," I compliment her, only for her to raise a middle finger over her shoulder as her head stays in the toilet.

"Horseradish sauce over the roast," she chokes out. "That cookbook my mother gave me as a wedding present said to use that."

"Ummm, sounds spicy," I reply, not sure what to say.

"The smells—oh, all day the smell. I haven't even kept water down."

Grabbing a hair tie from the countertop, I fumble to get her hair snug behind her. Once secured, I drop to my knees behind her and wrap my arms around her waist.

"I'm sorry, Mary Alice."

"No more kids," she mutters as she seems to settle down. "This is all you get."

If I had known pregnancy would be this hard on

her, I would have been okay to not have any. She's been miserable and happy all wrapped in one.

Standing, I get her a cup of water to rinse her mouth, which she does before flushing the toilet. Then I leave her to clean up privately, listening to her brushing her teeth as I walk out of the room. I can only hope turning off the dinner will help the smell pass so she won't continue to be sick.

In the kitchen, I butter some bread to go with the roast she made as well as make some toast for her. After grabbing a cold glass of water, I then plate the toast and take it into our bedroom.

"I can't eat with you tonight, Rhett," she groans out as she looks up from the bed. Her hands rest on her round belly. I see the puffiness in her eyes from crying through her times of sickness today.

"It's okay, baby. You didn't have to cook. I told you to take it easy."

"Promise me, Rhett. No more babies. I love you, and I love our baby, but I can't do this again," she pleads.

"If that's what you want," I concede. Hell, I would promise her the world if I could ease her burden right now and have my wife back.

After I set the toast on the nightstand beside her, she smacks my arm. "Are you blind? I can't eat that!"

"I thought—" I stammer. "I thought the doctor said eat toast."

"Have you seen my ass since I got pregnant?"

Smiling, I respond, "Sure have."

She smacks my arm again, letting me know she doesn't agree with my pleasure.

"Baby, you got ass and curves, and I love it. I can't help it if you turn me on."

She blinks. "I still turn you on?" The tears fall from her face.

I sit on the bed beside her. Reaching out, using the pad of my thumbs, I wipe the liquid from under her eyes. "You have always been the sexiest woman alive to me. Now you have these curves, and I look at you and know it's my seed growing inside you. Baby, nothing could be hotter. The way you love me keeps my dick hard." I lean over her and trail kisses on her chin. "Always hard for you."

"You," she whispers, "haven't been home as much."

"I'm an ass. God, I'm an ass." I press my lips to hers and taste the salt of her tears along with the mint of toothpaste. "Along with that ass has come a whole lot of sass. It's not you, baby," I say each word against her lips. "I just feel helpless, and you are miserable."

"I miss you."

"I'm right here, and I promise you no more running away. I'm with you every step of the way. No more horseradish smells making you sick without me here to hold your hair."

She laughs and I kiss her, taking the opportunity to slip my tongue inside and find hers. She brings her hands up to my hair and tugs as I deepen the kiss.

"Need to feel you," she says, pulling away to catch her breath.

After pulling off my shirt, I throw it to the side as I stand to remove my pants and socks. She slides her pants and panties off as I walk to the other side of the bed to climb in. Sliding her shirt over her belly, I kiss each side of it as I feel the telltale thump of our child kicking her.

"Daddy's gonna give momma some lovin', little one. Go to sleep," I whisper to her belly, making Mary Alice laugh.

She sits up so I can take her shirt off, and then I unhook her bra. When her ample breasts fall out in front of me, I nibble before sucking her nipple in deep, and she moans in pleasure. I then slide my hand between her legs. My fingers find her heat dripping wet as I slip two right in, and she cries out for more.

As she clenches around my digits, I pull out and

roll her to her side, settling in behind her. With one hand under her and tweaking her nipple, I use my other hand to lift her leg before guiding my rock hard dick into her from behind. She pushes her hips back as her inner muscles tighten and release around me while I fight the urge to release.

I bite at her neck and suck as I find her clit with my hand. I begin teasing, circling, and then pressing the bud as I slide in and out with her back to my chest, causing me to hit her spot with every thrust, making her whole body tremble as her orgasm overtakes her. Riding through the aftershocks, I find my own release.

Dinner forgotten, toast forgotten, everything comes together as I hold my woman in my arms, both of us completely satisfied.

A DOLL

ROUNDMAN

"Hush, little baby, don't say a word," Dia sings softly to our baby girl. "Daddy's gonna buy you a Harley shirt."

I can't stop the laugh that escapes as I lean against the doorjamb.

Little noises come from our baby, and Dia looks up at me with sharp eyes.

"Well then, Mister Chuckles, you come put her to sleep." She stands from the rocking chair and brings me the baby all wrapped in red.

Claudia was adamant that our nursery and baby not look like someone vomited Pepto pink in her room and her wardrobe. Can't say that I'm sad she feels that way, either.

With her hair all wild around her face, her eyes tired from lack of sleep these last few days, and baby spit-up on her shirt, my wife has never looked more disheveled nor more beautiful.

Taking Delilah from her arms, I kiss my wife on her forehead. "Go shower and take a nap, love."

"Gladly," she says with an exhausted smile. With a quick kiss to our daughter's head and one to my lips, she heads off to her sanctuary—our bedroom.

Sitting in the rocker that faces my daughter's crib all decked out in hot air balloons with teddy bears, I have to smile at how life has changed from the moment they placed Delilah in my arms.

With the face of a doll, eyes of an angel, and a head of blonde hair to match her mother's, my baby girl is absolutely perfect.

Bright eyes look up at me as she opens and closes her mouth like a fish. "Never known love so deep, dollface." My voice is raspy as I try not to be loud, but I want to talk to my little girl. "Loved your momma before, but watching her with you, holding you, having you … Well, Doll, I've never know anything purer in my life."

My daughter smiles. Dia says it's gas, but I don't care. My baby girl smiles before her eyes close, and she snuggles closer to me.

"Leather, oil, and man," I explain happily. "One day, you're gonna grow up, and when you find a man, he should smell like a hardworking man, Doll." The thought of my baby girl growing up has me twitching to shoot something. "Never mind that, precious. I promise you, as your dad, I'll be the man you look up to. I'll be the man who makes you proud. I'll be rock solid for you and your momma. I'll give you my all and my love." I rock her, thinking of what it's going to be like to watch her grow. "When the time comes to let you go, I'm going to fight like hell to keep you with me. I'll give my life before I'll let anyone touch you." Kissing her head as she soundly sleeps, I hold my daughter in my arms.

———

Eight weeks later, my balls are so tight I think they may bust. Between Dia healing from having our baby to the exhaustion we feel as new parents, there has been no time for the two of us to be, well, the two of us.

Leaving work, I'm dirty, tired, and I want nothing more than to kiss my Doll, kiss my wife, and go to sleep.

I pull up to our little trailer and park my bike then make my way inside. When there is no noise, I make sure to remove my boots without a sound to avoid waking my wife or my daughter.

At the kitchen sink, I wash my hands, splashing some water on my face before grabbing a beer from the fridge. When I make my way into the bedroom to change my clothes, I'm blown away.

Lying on our bed in a red lace number is my wife, Claudia Reklinger. Her breasts still swollen from having a baby, her tummy now flat, and her tone legs stretched out. I stand in the doorway and give a whistle, which makes her smile.

She curls a finger for me to come over, and stripping as I go, I slide in over her. My long hair in a braid falls over my shoulder and tickles the exposed skin of her collarbone. I kiss her briefly before I move slowly down her body, kissing and licking every available inch.

At her belly, I trace her stretch marks with my tongue, knowing it was my baby that grew in her body. I forever marked her in the way she forever marked my heart, stretching me to a new capacity to love I never knew possible.

With my teeth, I tug at her panties as she grips my hair in anticipation. I run my nose through her curls, inhaling the scent of her arousal, as I use my hands to slide her panties all the way off.

From her ankle to her inner thigh, I lick and tease her with my teeth. At her juncture, I flick my tongue against her glistening lips, lapping up every drop of her desire and settling in to feast. Claudia shamelessly grinds against my face.

Adding two fingers, I work in and out as I let my goatee tickle the sensitive skin between her folds before I suck deeply on her clit, sending her over the edge. Then I kiss my way up her body and slide my hard cock inside her while she milks me in her aftershocks.

Resting my forehead on hers, I still. "Baby, you're gonna make me blow too fast."

"Sugar, I'm just glad to know I can still make you go."

As I kiss her, I taste her arousal, my beer, and the mint of toothpaste as I try to calm myself. "Love you, Dia. It's only you. Women can wind me up, baby, but it's always going to be you who keeps me fighting the edge just so I can have more. A lifetime deep inside you isn't enough."

"Then love me for eternity, Blaine."

"Damn right," I whisper, sliding in and out of my wife.

A lifetime deep inside her isn't enough. I mean every word. I'll proudly love this woman for eternity.

CHAPTER TWELVE

BARBECUE

FRISCO

ONE YEAR LATER

The problem with not having a family of your own is feeling left out when your Hellions' brothers have all started their own. I hate to admit it, but I can't shake the sadness that I'm not in the same place they are. Then again, I have only one person to blame—me.

For too many years, I stayed on the road, going

from one place to another, taking on odd jobs here and there to get by but never settling in.

The Hellions changed all that for me. Here, I feel like I'm part of something. Here, I feel like I belong. Seeing the love between Danza and Mary Alice, Rocky and Marie, Roundman and Dia, it makes me wonder if I'm missing out by just having a mindless fuck with a barfly.

Growing up, my mom and I lived under a bridge in the Bay area. She was a meth addict who only worked odd jobs to cover her next high. I only went to school so I could get free lunch. I wore the same clothes day in and out, my baths taken in the cold bay water. Kids teased me mercilessly, but I prevailed.

When my mom died, I was only fifteen. No one knew; no one cared. I found her body in our blanket under the bridge and left her there, moving on to start squatting in foreclosed houses.

I got myself a job as a busboy at a restaurant. The owners, Shipley Pete and his wife, soon figured out my secret and let me move into their son's old bedroom. Having a safe place to stay, clothes on my back, and being able to clean up, I was doing good.

After I saved up, Shipley sold me his Harley. Learning to ride, feeling the freedom, gave me the escape from life. Then, when Shipley had his heart attack and his wife moved to Washington with their son, I hit the road and didn't look back.

I was lost until I landed in Haywood's Landing with the Hellions. The guys took me in without questioning my past or judging me.

I never imagined having a family of my own, but with the club, I have one, and now I can't help wondering if I dare to have more.

"Been thinking," Roundman says, walking into the client waiting area of his bike shop.

"You have a brain?" Danza teases his long-time friend.

"Shut up, fucker."

"Whatcha thinkin', brother?" Rocky, the more serious of us all, asks.

"We should have a barbecue out back here. We've built around the shop; we have the clubhouse; we have the cave; so now let's have a backyard barbecue. We can have our ol' ladies out with the kids, make it a real family thing."

A family thing. I rub my chest absently, an ache burning inside.

"We're a family of our own making. I say, hell yeah," Danza chimes in.

Rocky nods his agreement, and Roundman looks at me.

"Well, let's get to work. We have to get some grills and some tables," I say.

Roundman gives me a smirk. "California kid, we gotta build a Carolina-style pig cooker."

Rocky is the first to move out the front door. "Let's get to it."

Within an hour, we are cutting, welding, and creating our own charcoal grill, cut out of a burn barrel. We make the shell of the whole hog cooker and add the hinges to make the top and bottom seal up but still have slats for the metal grates that will hold the hog in place.

For three days, we work on cookers and grills before moving on to tables. We make custom twelve-foot family style tables and even go so far as make a few square cut-outs edged with stainless steel. Once we toss a bucket under the holes, we have the perfect oyster-shucking tables for oyster roasts when the season comes.

Excitement fills me at the prospect of having these memories with my club. Then, at the same time, I feel like something is missing. They have their women and now their kids. Just like my childhood, I'm alone under the bridge.

Within a week, we have everything set up and food bought. Dia, Mary Alice, and Marie are making side items while we'll man the grills. Roundman has invited all patched members and their families, and it's not long before the party is in full swing. The kids are playing, the beer is getting guzzled, and the women are happily on their men's arms.

Marie brought a new friend she met at the craft store the other day. As I run my fingers over my goatee, my mouth waters at the beauty in front of me. She has this shy look that only intrigues me more. In her mini-skirt, her legs go on for miles, and I can't stop myself from imagining them wrapped around my neck while I eat her pussy like it's my last meal. The woman has hair the color of molasses, and it's in a kinky curl that makes me wonder what kind of kink she would be into with me.

Strolling over, I give her my smile, and she looks around as if I'm looking at someone else.

"What's your name, pretty thing?"

Marie laughs yet doesn't introduce us.

"Tilly," she says barely above a whisper.

I tip her chin to make her look me in the eye. "I'm Frisco."

That's when the fire comes alive between us. Her eyes dance in mischief and, dare I let myself believe, lust.

"Frisco isn't a name. What's your name?"

It's been a long time since anyone cared to know Richard. My life has been about the club and my role in the club for so long I find her interest refreshing.

"Richard Billings."

She extends her hand for me to shake, but instead, I press my luck, dropping my lips to touch hers. There is a spark and a sizzle, only making me need to have this woman more.

I never expected for this barbecue to be so fun. I never expected to meet anyone who would spark my interest for more than the time it takes for me to get off. Tilly is different, and she challenges me. I get off on a challenge.

Keep it coming, baby.

DOING TIME

ROUNDMAN

TWO YEARS LATER

I should have known the first time we got pulled over that something wasn't right. Danza wasn't speeding, the truck was up to code, and all the plates were good. There was no reason for the first cop to pull us over.

Hell, the really fucked up part is I wasn't supposed to take the run at all.

Frisco got himself a woman, Matilda, some time

ago. Well, Tilly called this morning as he was about to roll out with Danza to say she had to go to the hospital. Dia offered to take her, but she said she needed Frisco, that it was a private matter. Assuming she had womanly issues, my woman told me to stand down and take the ride-along while Frisco took care of what's his.

I can stand behind that. If it were my woman and she was sick in any way, I would want to be with her, not in some rig on the highway.

We aren't an hour passed the last place we got pulled when I see blue lights in the mirror again.

"Danza, we got company," I inform.

"I see 'em," he says as he brings the rig to the side of the road.

After I hand him the log books, the registration, and insurance, he reaches in his wallet for his license. Then he rolls the window down, and we wait.

Automatically with our hands in the air so the officer doesn't get trigger happy, we allow him to open the driver door to the rig.

"Need you to open the trailer," he automatically orders.

My suspicions rise.

"Mind telling me what we got pulled over for?" I ask. "We have a deadline."

"Got reasonable cause. A truck matching this description came in on the scanner as reported stolen. I have to match your load and registration to your logs and search to make sure this isn't the load reported."

I look at Danza. *Someone called in a stolen transport that just happens to fit the description of our rig?* This doesn't sit right with me.

He gives me a slight shrug of his shoulders as we clamber out of the truck. We both know what's back there. We both hope like hell he doesn't do a deep search.

We are both up a creek without a paddle.

Two hours later, the rig is impounded, and Danza and I sit behind bars. The tiny town we're in isn't the least bit concerned with rights, schedules, or a damn thing we have going on at home.

We are given one phone call for the two of us. We need to make it count.

"Rocky," I say quickly when he answers the shop phone. "Danza and I are in lock-up. Need you to handle shit."

With his affirmation, I hang up and am taken back to the holding cell.

ROCKY

"Hello," Claudia answers, and I hear little Delilah in the background.

"It's Rocky," I explain. "Roundman and Danza have a delay."

"What kind of delay?" There is worry in her voice, and I don't like it.

"The kind that may take a while," I tell her honestly.

"They okay?"

"Yeah, just gonna be gone for a while. If you need anything, I'm here."

"Mary Alice know yet?"

"That's my next call."

Claudia, being the strong woman she is, says, "I'll handle it."

"I appreciate it."

Hanging up the receiver, dread fills my gut. Our top two in lock up for God knows how long is the last thing we need right now.

I spend the day tightening things up at the shop and getting an attorney for the guys.

If the situation were reversed, the two of them would have my back and my family's. I'll do the same. Too bad none of us could have predicted the future to know just how deep we were. Trouble is funny like that, though. You never know how much you're in until you're there.

———

The gavel crashes down in the courtroom. Claudia jumps up and rushes to Roundman to give him a kiss on the cheek as the deputy comes over to escort him to the jail before his transport to the state penitentiary. Mary Alice twists her hands nervously from her seat but doesn't move as Danza calls out to her. She looks up slowly, sad eyes meeting my brother's as he is guided from the room without his wife moving an inch. I give the ladies a few moments to collect themselves before I clear my throat, signaling we should leave.

After loading them up in my car, we make our way silently back to Haywood's Landing. The weight of the club rests on my shoulders. Frisco and I have to step up while Roundman and Danza serve their time. The club has expanded into central and western North Carolina, and we even have a few charters in South Carolina now. I'll need to get in touch with all our charter presidents to make them aware of the final verdict.

Leaving Claudia with Mary Alice, I drive home instead of to the shop. Marie opens the front door before I can even reach it.

"You okay, Tommy?" she asks me in the tender way that simply is my wife.

"Been better, baby." I step into our home and go to the couch to take off my boots.

Marie sits down next to me. "How bad is it?"

I let out a huff. "Three years."

Softly, she places her hands on the back of my neck. "You can do this. You can hold things down for them. If the situation were reversed, they would take care of me, Dina, and all of your obligations." She smiles sweetly. "It's the way you Hellions are: trouble making, love making rebels with a heart for family."

Leaning over, I place my lips against hers. "Damn, I'm a lucky man."

"I'm the lucky one," she says against my lips. "I believe in you, Tommy. I always have, even when you were the smelly boy next-door, climbing trees. Every time you fell over the fence, I knew you would get back up and do it again the next day."

I laugh. "I was doing that in hopes of getting your attention. Instead, I got your daddy yelling about me making a mess in your yard with the leaves and broken branches."

"You tell a lie, Tommy Fowler! You didn't even know I existed. You were hoping you would see my sister Becky in her bathing suit."

I lift my hands in surrender. "Busted. But, baby, you should know, now that I've seen all you kept hidden just for me, your sister ain't never had shit on you."

"I love you, Tommy. You, Blaine, and Rhett have been the three amigos since we were kids. We'll get through this together like everything else."

"I love you, Marie. Thank you for having faith in me and my club."

"As Claudia says, ride until we die, baby."

———

They spend three years locked up in the state jail for possession with intent to distribute across state lines. Mary Alice had a rough time of it early on, but she's strong. Claudia and she moved in together for a bit to help each other with the babies growing up.

The club now has an attorney who said it would be in our best interests to separate the businesses. Haywood's Landing now has my car restoration and mechanics shop down the street from what was once Clive's and is now Roundman's bike shop. Claudia and he are building a house on the lot next door so the property is expanded.

Mary Alice doesn't want Danza on the road anymore. I told her he could work for me since Frisco has been running the bike shop while Roundman was away.

While they were locked up, we managed to build a real clubhouse and grow the Hellions MC. We are stronger than ever before, even though Fury MC has kept their distance.

The day they rolled in on Clive is one that is forever engrained in my memory. I will never forget the fear I felt, the helplessness that consumed me as I was left with no choice but to take a life in order to save that of my friend and myself.

We are family. Through thick and thin, we hold each other up.

DANZA

D ear Rhett,
   I know you expected me to visit today and bring Savannah. I can't. I just can't do this anymore. The time is nearing for you to return home, and I'll be honest with you and myself, I don't think you should come to our house. You see, while you've been serving your time, so have we. You see, while you've been away, I've been okay on my own. Rocky, Frisco, and all the club have stepped in during your absence, but more than that, I've learned to stand on my own without you. I've learned not to wait for hours on end for you to pull in to our driveway. I haven't had to spend my time wondering if you would come home or if you would pick a fight with me just to have an excuse to leave.

This is the hardest decision I've ever had to make, but for me and my daughter, I'm asking you to go to the compound and not here. I'm asking that you let me go.

I've stood by you through everything. I've done anything asked of me. Now I ask of you to please make this easy and let me go.

You will always have my heart, but I cannot continue to remain numb to the pain you continue to bring me. I will love you with every breath I take, but I need the same from you.

I want a life with mutual respect, adoration, and emotion through the good and the bad. If you can't give me that, then at least give me the freedom to be on my own rather than wait around for you to have an epiphany that will never come.

With love and tears,

Mary Alice

Three weeks until I get out of this place and this is what she sends me.

I punch the brick wall of my cell, and Roundman stands and comes to me.

"Wanna tell me what that's about, brother?"

"Not gonna let her go," I growl.

"Then you better straighten out your shit, brother."

I let my mind go over all the wrongs I've done. The first time I stepped out on her, I told myself it was just to have something new. Mary Alice was my first everything. I knew it was wrong, but each and every time I let a barfly touch me, I found some way to justify it to myself. There is no justification. I'm wrong. I have taken for granted the gift of her love. I have expected her loyalty without giving it in return. I have left my woman and our child while I serve time and really not given a second thought to what it has done to her. Well, I see clearly now. I've done wrong, but all is not lost.

This isn't the end, Mary Alice. I've made mistakes, but I can't walk away.

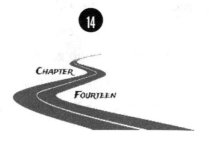

HOMECOMING

FRISCO

The guys are getting released this morning. We are giving them the day with their women so they can get laid. Tonight, though, it's a party at the compound where Rocky and I took the time to build a stage and get a band to come out to play.

I never thought about how hard it is to balance a family and the club. I don't know how the guys do it plus have kids. Hell, I never really expected to settle down anywhere. Something from the beginning tied me to the guys, though.

Rhett and I met on the side of the highway in Alabama. He said if I was ever in North Carolina, Blaine's shop was the place to get my bike serviced. I had nowhere else to be, no place to call home, or family to worry about, so the coast sounded pretty nice to me.

I didn't expect to ride in and make it a permanent home. I definitely didn't expect to bond with these men as if they were my blood brothers. More than that, I didn't think I could find a woman I wanted to spend more time with than the energy it took to get off.

Then I met Matilda. She's fire and ice all in one. She winds me up and sets me off more than any other human. We have this crazy pull between us. I've never had someone want me and only me the way this woman does.

Tilly rides my ass so hard about not being home enough without them. She needs more support. If I'm not at work, she wants me in her pussy.

Don't get me wrong, I love her pussy, but come on; a man needs a break. Truth be told, I don't even think the woman does it for the orgasms as much as she does it to keep control of my balls. If I'm in her, then I'm not anywhere else. Swear to Christ, I think, if she could sleep with my limp dick inside her, she would just so she could sleep and not think I'm going to sneak out or something crazy like that.

It's not long after we get the party started that Roundman and Danza arrive with their women at their sides.

My woman, she's giving the lead singer of some shit-ass band a good look down her cleavage. Where is the love? Where is the loyalty?

My anger boils.

Stepping out back, I go to the makeshift horseshoe area we have, throwing back a beer before picking up the metal set to toss. Slice comes over with another beer in his hand for me and the other set of shoes.

"You all right, brother?" he asks.

"Wanna fuckin' cut the broad loose. Can't seem to shake her, though. When it's me and her, she's a fuckin' dream. The second there is anyone or anything else going on besides me being with her, then all hell breaks loose."

Slice laughs as he tips his beer up.

Rocky strolls over, saying, "Pussy on the regular can't be that bad, especially if she ain't wantin' the house, the kids, the fucking station wagon, and the dog."

"Oh, but she is," I reply, feeling the weight of my situation on me.

"Frisco!" Tilly calls out to me. "California kid, if you won't love me right, this one will."

Rage runs through me. I want to beat that fucker's ass as my woman reaches up and grabs his dick. At the same time, I want to fuck her into oblivion so she will shut the hell up.

Everything happens in a blur, and before I realize it, I have beaten the hell out of the lead singer of the band. With blood on my knuckles, anger in my eyes, my brothers all at my back, Tilly looks at me with love.

"Shit's fucked up, Tilly."

"Choose me, Frisco."

I shake my head, blood pouring from my busted lip. "Come again?"

"Choose me," she whispers before she turns and walks away.

I let her go. Stupidly, I let her go.

With every fiber of my being, I know she wants me to follow her. I know she needs me to choose her over the mayhem of the night. I know her heart craves my attention. Everything inside me screams to follow that tail right out the doors and don't look back.

After all, I am a man. We tend to get led around

by our dicks. My dick knows that me throwing down for her ensures she's going to ride me hard and long tonight.

The problem is that's what she wants all the time. Everything is a choice: her pussy or …

Her pussy is tired. Her mouth is tired. I'm so sick of the break up to make up I can't see straight.

What's worse? My brothers have come home from doing time, and I've gone and beaten the hell out of some shit-ass band all because of tired, worn out pussy.

There is something wrong with me. Seriously fucking wrong with me, because even in all this, for a moment, a brief moment, I considered following that pussy right out the door.

Thankfully, I used my brain for once.

Looking around, I see the clubhouse is a wreck. Roundman is smiling before devouring Dia in a kiss while Danza looks like he's on the prowl. Both men were big before their years of three hots and a cot, but the time in the yard has seriously bulked the two of them up.

Going to Danza first, I extend my hand. "Sorry about the mess, brother."

He grabs mine in a firm hold. "Nothin' to be sorry 'bout, man. Fucker had it comin'. If it were my woman, I'd have made him choke on his own balls."

"Your woman wouldn't have given that man a second look."

With a cocky smile, Danza nods. "You got a crazy one, Frisco."

He's right about that.

I take my time cleaning up the clubhouse and making sure everything gets squared away. It is my fault things got out of hand tonight; it's the least I could do. A smart man would have either followed his woman out of the clubhouse hours before or kept his ass with his club.

I'm a man, but I'm not always a smart man.

Finally pulling up to the single-wide trailer Tilly and I share, I should have known things were different this time when I didn't find my shit in the front yard. In all the time we've gone back and forth, I swear she has put me out more times than years we've been together.

Walking in, the lights are off except in the bedroom. As I enter the space, the sight in front of me has my guts in knots.

On our bed, naked with cuts all over her body and blood still running out of her, lies Tilly.

"Baby!" I call out, rushing over to her.

With her eyes closed, I make the mistake of assuming she's passed out from blood loss.

This isn't the first mistake I've made where this woman is concerned.

The sharp metal hits my throat as her wild eyes pop open.

"Told you," she says with a rasp to her voice like she's been screaming for hours on end. "Begged you. How many times have I gotten on my knees and begged you to choose me! Me!" she screams as the blade cuts into my skin.

I don't move. I should. I should break her fucking wrist and take the knife. I should pull my gun from my back and shoot her in the head. Yet, I don't.

Instead, I take the pain as the burn hits when the opening of my wound is exposed to the air. I don't stop her as I let the crazed woman in front of me find her twisted pleasure in watching my neck bleed.

"You feel powerful now, Tilly?" I ask as she presses harder into my skin.

"More than ever before."

"Taking my life mean that much to you?"

"You're mine, Richard. You always go where the club needs you, but what about me? What about *us*? I've tried everything, yet you always choose the club."

"What's this, Tilly? If you can't have me, no one can?"

She pauses at my words. At the nod of her head, I know I'm fucked.

Reaching up, I take her wrist in mine as the metal digs in. Then I yank hard, and she yelps as I twist, forcing her to release the weapon.

Tears stream down her face, falling to her naked torso and mixing with the blood where she's sliced herself.

"I had a plan," she whispers.

"I can see that."

"Gonna take you out, say it was self-defense."

My heart hurts for the pain I've given this woman. This is the moment when I should have known better. She isn't strong enough for the life I live. She isn't ready to have times when I can't share things with her —not because I don't want to, but because it's in her best interest. I have broken this beautiful woman, all because I do choose the Hellions.

"Tilly, I'm gonna release you. I'm gonna climb on my bike and never look back. I should kill you for what you've done, but I'm simply gonna walk away."

"Kill me!" she screeches. "Just do it! You already killed me on the inside."

"I know," I give her solemnly. "I never intended

to. I'm gonna get you set up financially for a while. When you're straight, you move on. There's a good woman inside you, the kind of woman who could make a lot of men happy."

"Just not you," she says quietly.

"Not a man like me, no. Go on with life, Tilly. Instead of me choosing you, *you* choose you. Gonna go now. Don't try to stab me in the back. This is our time to part ways."

I expect her to jump me. I anticipate the move. She never does.

I leave the trailer like I said and don't look back. I go to the one place that really is home—the Hellions' compound.

Sometimes, love lost is love won. One day, Tilly will realize this when she wins her happiness away from me and my club.

LOSING IT ALL

ROUNDMAN

SEVEN YEARS LATER

"Fuck cancer! Fuck it all!" I roar, throwing the beer bottle at the wall behind the bar and watching the glass shatter.

My wife is at home, painting Delilah's toenails, while I try to wrap my head around the fact that the treatment failed. My beautiful wife, my strong, vibrant woman, has months left. It isn't supposed to be like this.

I have spent the last year holding her hand while she has been in pain so bad she can't move. I have watched her cry as her hair, her beautiful blonde hair, fell out chunk by chunk. I continuously sat in the waiting room of the hospital as she had the surgery to remove her breasts. Her beautiful breasts are no more.

All because of fucking cancer.

Through it all, through every high and every low, Dia has been strong. She has smiled through the pain, laughed during the agony, and pushed through each and every day, only to find out that we are once again losing the battle.

I feel like I'm dying inside. The mere thought of one day, one minute without her by my side is a hell unlike any other.

Send me back to jail, brand me with a hot iron, cut my dick off and shove it up my ass, but God, please don't take her from me.

A slap on my shoulder has me turning my head.

"Let it out here, brother," Danza says. "Let the walls have it all. Then take your ass home, and Roundman, you give her every part of you left to give until the very end."

Blinking, I jump up and head home. I don't want to waste time. I don't want to be away from her.

Once our little Doll is fast asleep, I climb into bed

beside my wife. Her eyes don't hide the pain, the fatigue, or the sadness she's carrying around.

Laying my head on her chest, I listen to the steady thumping of her heartbeat.

"Blaine," she whispers as she strokes my hair. "Sugar, times a comin'. Doll's gonna need you."

With no shame, I let the tears fall. "Can't do it without you. I'm a man, baby; how can I be what she needs as a girl?"

"You are what she needs because, love, you have always been exactly what I needed when I needed it. Ain't nobody stronger, more loyal, and more loving than you."

"You're wrong." I hold her tightly, hating feeling her frail body under me yet selfishly needing to hear the *thump, thump, thump* of her life moving through her body. "You're the strongest person I know."

"Blaine, I'm always with you. Eternity, baby, I promise you. I'll love you for eternity. We have a girl, a beautiful, magical, wonderful little girl, and she's gonna need you."

I lift my head and look into her eyes. "I could get lost in the depths of your eyes."

"We gotta face this. Gotta be prepared."

Sliding up, I rest my forehead against hers. "I can't let you go, Claudia. Don't ask me to let you go."

Before she can answer, I press my lips to hers to keep her quiet. I can't let her say the words. I can't hear her tell me to go on.

Breaking away, I brush my lips to hers again. "You are my partner. You are my lifeline. You are my heart." I kiss her deeply again. "Made you promises, baby. Dia, I gave you my word. It's ride beyond this lifetime, you and me. Don't give up on me, because I damn sure ain't giving up on you."

Bracing my weight on my forearm, I tenderly rub the soft skin of her scalp where her hair once was. Then I close my eyes, and my tears fall down her face, mixing with her own as I remember the times I would brush her hair from her eyes.

I kiss her forehead then under each eye, tasting the salt of her tears. Then I kiss her nose and each cheek before I once again press my lips to hers.

She holds me to her, and I feel the strain as she tries to grip me more firmly.

"Love me, Blaine," she whispers against my lips.

"For all my days, Claudia, and beyond," I tell her before I slowly, softly, and with every bit of my soul make love to my wife for the last time.

IT TAKES A CLUB

ROUNDMAN

L aying my wife to rest is the hardest thing I've ever had to do.

I think back to the day I killed the men of Fury MC. Is this my karma? Is this my punishment?

The loss of the love I'll never share again kills me little bit by little bit.

Yet, for our daughter, I have to hold strong.

Delilah is the best part of Claudia and me. She is a physical piece of our love coming together. She is what I can hold on to when I need to remember what I had.

People say I should move on. Even before my wife died, the barflies were ready to pounce. There is no moving on for me, though. Claudia stood by me when a million other women would have left. I will not tarnish her memory by putting anyone else in her place. She is my heart, my soul, and will always be my wife.

"She loved you," Mary Alice whispers, placing a gentle hand on my shoulder. "Blaine"—she pauses —"she *loves* you."

I turn to my wife's best friend and see the tears in her eyes as she hands me an envelope.

"Take a moment for yourself. I'll be in the kitchen, setting out food and making sure Doll's hanging in there."

Sitting on the edge of my bed, the bed I made love to my wife in so many times before and never will again, I trace the edge of the envelope. In her script is my name on the outside with the simple note, *For when the time comes that I am here no more.*

Blowing out a breath, I open the last gift from my wife.

Inhaling, I smell the faint scent of her perfume.

Then I unfold the paper and treasure the curves of every letter.

My vision blurs as the tears once again fill my eyes.

Squeezing them shut, I pinch the bridge of my nose and hold them back as I read:

Blaine,

My badass bear, we go back so far I don't remember a time in my life without you in it.

Every tear I've cried in the last few months has been for the things I will miss with you and Delilah.

Our ride has been paved in rough patches, ups, downs, good times, and sometimes painful times. Do not cry for me, Blaine. Do not cry for a loss, because the love we share crosses all time, all distance, and it's a kind few get to experience.

Being sick hasn't been easy for you, me, or our little girl. You have been my rock and my soft place to fall all in one when it got bad.

As my body changed, as my hair fell out, as I slept more than I could stay awake, you have been there to tell me you find me beautiful, and your love for me never once wavered. As I write this, I know the time is coming when I will be here no more. Knowing you will be reading this once I'm gone, I need you to know, Blaine, I love you, and it hasn't wavered once since our first kiss. You have given me life, love, and happiness.

Our Doll, a gift so precious I still can't believe she's ours. I wish I could hold your hand as she grows the way you held mine when she was born.

Baby, you have a tough road ahead of you, but there isn't anyone stronger in this whole world than you. I need you to hold our little girl tight ... but when the time comes, I trust you'll know I need you to let her go.

My dream for Delilah is to have a love like ours. When the man comes along who is strong enough to stand before you and claim her, you'll know it's my blessing you are giving with your own. As much as your instincts will scream to keep her close, she's a wild one, our baby girl, and you'll need to let her run at times.

Raising kids is never easy. Raising a girl into a woman as a man isn't going to be any easier. I need you to remember something, Blaine.

It takes a club.

No matter what this life throws at you until I see you again, my love, remember it takes a club. The Hellions have your back. They have our daughter's back. Let them hold you up when you feel down.

You are a good man, Blaine Reklinger, and even

though at times it may feel like it, you are not alone. You have the Hellions, and baby, you have my heart.

My dream for the club is to be a family. It's not always blood that connects you; it's bond, it's life, it's love, and it's loss. Grow the Hellions beyond Haywood's Landing.

In this crazy chaos, find a way to give people a safe place to become good men like you. Control what you can and leave the rest to the club to keep everyone in the right place.

My love, my dream for you is to let go of the things that hold you back. The past is in the past, baby, and sometimes, as much as it hurts, we have to let go.

Leaving you behind hurts my mind, my heart, and deep into my soul. You are the half that makes me whole. I have to say good-bye, but only in space and time, because I'm always in your heart, Blaine.

Please don't let this time apart harden you. Be open to whatever life throws you. Do not become bitter; do not become harsh. Be the Blaine I fell in love with and the man you are today so that our daughter can still experience what makes you, you and what made us, us.

I will see you again one day, my love. Until then, kiss our daughter's head and tell her I'm in her heart.

*Love without hesitation, laugh without reserve, and
baby, live without a single regret.*

   All my love for always and into eternity,

   Your wife, Claudia Reklinger

I hear the sounds of my house filling with people.
The sounds of mourning, or as Dia chose for us to call
it, her celebration of life. I can't celebrate her loss as
much as she wants me to. I can't avoid dwelling on
the fact that, three days ago, she took her last breath,
and from that moment on, I have not been able to
look forward to the end of a day anymore. There is
nothing to look forward to for me beyond our
daughter.

   For fifteen years, I have lain in bed beside her
except the time I was locked up. I haven't slept since
she's passed on.

   How can I?

   My first thought, *It takes a club.*

   Hearing the rumble of more bikes pulling in
somehow soothes the ache that is deep inside me. Dia
is right: *It takes a club.*

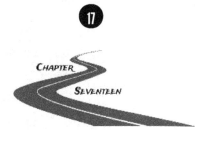

CRASH

ROCKY

THREE YEARS LATER

For the first time in a long time, things are solid. Business is good, the club is good, and life is damn good.

Honestly, I never would have thought Marie and I would have made it this far. Yet, we're still together, and our little girl Dina is off to college. The empty nest has only made my wife want to do more things with me, like car shows. We now live in a nice beach house; that was her dream.

With as much shit as she has put up with over the years, I'll give her a mansion in Malibu if that's what she wants, even if it kills me to make the payment. In the end, she doesn't want any of that, though; she simply wants me and the life we have together.

Today, we're on our way to a Mustang show for her. I'm a Chevy bowtie man, but she's a "wild horses have to run" kind of woman. Secretly, I think she loves her Mustangs just to challenge me. Some couples have competing football teams; we like different brands for our rides. It keeps it fresh.

Dina usually would go with us, but being in Charlotte, she has college life and better things to do.

Roundman, being the good friend he is, made sure we expanded the club to that area, starting a Catawba Hellions' charter. The guys there keep an eye on Dina and her best friend Maggie for us.

Family. We have all come from different walks and different backgrounds, but we managed to become the support system each of us has needed.

Roundman, Danza, Frisco, and I started something years ago for protection that has grown into a foundation for future generations to never be alone. Since Roundman and I separated the businesses, I have moved more to restoration projects, leaving the bikes and general car maintenance to him and the Hellions.

I think back to that day with Clive so long ago. If Blaine hadn't taken the lead that day, I can't say I would be here today. I don't know that I would have been able to think clear-headed enough to grab the weapons and fire to save myself and Clive.

Roundman has led the club from the ground up and into something that is not only solid, but also profitable. With each passing year, I find myself more thankful for what we have built in the Hellions.

I'm also thankful that, years ago, Marie took a chance to ride with me one night. Sure, I just wanted to have sex with her in the beginning, but over time, we built something more, something real. And here we are today, still strong, even if our start wasn't the thing they write romance stories about.

"Rocky," Marie says beside me over the rumble of her 'Stang.

"Yeah?"

"What's got you so lost in thought?"

I smile at the beautiful woman beside me. "Thinking about how far we've come."

She laughs. "The miles behind us only help us navigate the road ahead."

"I love you." I lean over and kiss her cheek before pulling out onto the highway.

With her hand in mine, we head home with our best in show trophy in the trunk. We had a damn good day, just the two of us.

The light is red up ahead, but the eighteen wheeler is sitting still and slightly back from the light. I can't help noticing it and wonder if he's broken down. I'm no diesel mechanic, but he's not in the best place to be stuck.

The light changes to green, so I keep the gas pedal down to go through just as I notice the truck moving again. *What the hell?* My mind races as I try to get us through safely.

Bright lights glare through the windows at us before I feel the clip of the truck to the back of the small car. My wife cries out as glass breaks around us and the car spins.

I drop her hand as I grip the steering wheel, trying to turn in the opposite direction to stop the rotation, but we roll. The metal continues to crunch around us as I hit my head on the roof, the lap belts doing nothing to secure either of us to the seats.

Marie reaches out, grabbing my hand, while I hold tightly to hers when the car stops.

"Love you, baby. You okay?" I ask her as pain shoots through my body.

We are both curled into the roof of the car that sits upside down. Our bodies are at unusual angles, and I immediately feel pain shoot through my legs, up my spine, and into my neck.

"It hurts," she whispers.

"I know, baby. I'm gonna get us out of here," I try to reassure her.

Turning my head as best I can, I look for exit strategies. Then we hear the truck coming toward us, and panic fills me as my wife cries out into the night.

The headlights shining in are blinding. The sounds of gears grinding echoes through the air as the rig comes closer and gains speed.

"I love you, Tommy," my wife's last words register at the same time the impact comes and darkness closes in on us both.

Thanks for standing by me, Marie, my love, is my last thought before I feel nothing anymore.

DANZA

How did it all go so wrong? It seems, every time we finally settle down, the bitch called life throws another curveball our way.

A drunk driver in a beverage distribution truck hit and killed Rocky and Marie Fowler.

Tommy-boy is gone. The man who has been by mine and Roundman's sides since elementary school isn't coming home. I can't think of a time when the three of us have been apart other than when Blaine and I served our time in jail and Rocky stepped up, taking care of our wives and girls while we sat in our cells, counting down the days.

Looking to the blue sky above, I say, "I promise you, brother, we're gonna make sure business is handled, and Dina is set for life. You took care of my house when I couldn't, and I'm gonna take care of yours." I toss a finger to the sky, giving my man my word.

I've done so much wrong over the years. Pain runs deeper inside me than I've ever let on. Secrets hold me back from being the man I should be, a man like Rocky was. Today, I change all that.

I owe my wife a lifetime of love, devotion, and no more messing things up for us. She's held me down when any other woman would have left. She deserves better than what she has in me, but I'm a selfish fuck who won't let her go, either.

When I step inside the home I share with Mary Alice, I hear the sounds of Sass giving her mother hell.

"I wanna go to Doll's, and you can't stop me," she says with every bit of attitude that gave her the nickname Sass. "It's to study. Dad isn't going to let me not have a study partner. He'll put you in your place, ol' lady."

I take a moment to think. She's right. Any other day, any other time, I would probably go inside and tell Mary Alice to let Savannah go. When she tried to protest, I would tell her I'm the man and I overrule her.

I'm a fucking ass is what I am.

Kicking my boots off at the front door, I stand there as my daughter's eyes come to me.

"Tell Mom I can go study."

Mary Alice looks down, avoiding me. She already assumes I'm going to give in to Sass. My wife has lost her fight.

I did this to her.

I've spent too many years on the road. For too many years, I've pushed her away. Too many mistakes have come between us, and she doesn't even know them all.

"Savannah, you need to tame your shit. You aren't going anywhere except to your room."

Mary Alice looks up at me with surprise in her eyes.

I simply nod at her so she silently knows I have her back.

Sass doesn't move, so I look at my teen daughter. "I'm not one for repeatin' myself."

She stomps off, and I fight the urge to yank her up for the disrespect. I have too much to handle with my wife to deal with the dramatics of a hormonal young woman.

"Mary Alice," I say, losing some of the confidence I had worked up to have this talk.

She makes her way to me, and I take her by the hand to guide her into our bedroom.

"Rhett, you're making me nervous," she tells me honestly as I point for her to sit on the bed.

Dropping to my knees in front of her, I hold nothing back. "I messed up, baby. I've messed up for a lot of damn years."

She cradles each side of my face with her soft hands, forcing me to look her in the eyes. "Tell me," she whispers with tears running down her cheeks. "Say the words; give me it all."

"You have been rock solid. You stood by me when everyone else would have left."

"Tell me, Rhett."

"I'm on my knees, Mary Alice. I'm on my knees to promise you I've changed."

"Say the words, Rhett Perchton. Tell me."

"It won't happen again. From this day forward, ride until we die, Mary Alice. I promise you." I choke on my emotions.

"Rhett," she whispers, "just say the words. Own it. I need you to give that to me. I need you to accept responsibility. I'm not crazy, it's not lost, and I didn't stay when everything told me to leave for nothing. Dammit, Rhett, tell me."

"I haven't kept my vows," I say the words,

forcing her hands off my face so I can drop my head and not watch her eyes as I kill the life we have built together.

Two soft hands grip my chin, forcing me to look at her again. I can't get a read on her because the tears are falling so fast, and she keeps blinking. I feel a slight tremble as she starts to speak then stops.

After a brief pause, she firmly tells me, "I already know."

I swear the world stops spinning.

"How?"

"A woman knows when her man ain't right. A woman knows when a man who's been good goes bad. I've known for a long time."

"Yet you've stayed."

"I gave my word, Rhett. Unlike some of us in the Perchton family, I keep it. I asked you to let me go. You came home from jail, and you said you would change. You said you didn't want to let me go. Why should you, really? I stayed and stayed, and even when I knew what a dirty bastard you were, I stuck by you. I kept my vows. I kept my love. I gave you my loyalty."

With those words, she guts me. Everything crashes around me.

Holding her face in my hands, my tear-filled eyes

meet hers. "I promise you with everything good we've ever shared and built together, no more fuck ups, Mary Alice. I give you my all. I know you don't believe it, but I've lost too much, and I won't lose you. Ride until we die, baby. I'm yours and no one else's. I love you, Mary Alice. I fucked up more than I can count, but believe me; I love you. I will spend the rest of the days we have together giving you everything I should have been giving you all along. I will have your back like you've had mine. I'm a changed man. Mary Alice, please give me a chance to show you."

She says nothing as I press my lips to hers. For what feels like a lifetime, she doesn't move. Then, finally, she wraps her arms around my neck and opens, pulling me to her.

Sealed with a kiss, I will give this woman everything she deserves and more from this day forward. With no excuses for my past and no cushion for my future, I will not fail her again.

Today, I lost a brother. It opened my eyes to everything I've done wrong over the years. I took the love of a once vibrant woman, and I slowly killed her, not with my words, but with my actions.

Over and over again, I could have made it right. I should have made things right. I didn't.

No, I failed. I failed my wife. I failed my family. In turn, I also failed my club.

PART THREE INTRODUCTION

PART THREE

OUT OF PRIDE...
IT COMES TO A HEAD

PRESENT

You've got to stand for something, as the saying goes, or you'll fall for anything. The Hellions have always and will always be about family, about taking a brother's back, even if the brother is no longer with us. Rocky stood by me through some of the hardest times in my life. His death will not go unpunished. Even if my pride alone causes me to fall, I do so with a fight for my brother's legacy.

~Roundman~

THREATS KEEP COMING

ROUNDMAN

W e have all filed into the cave for sermon. This is our patched members only meeting.

Tripp and Rex took a run for Ravage MC. In the process, we were tailed, but not over the transport.

Fury MC has decided their time has come.

It's been over twenty damn years since they rolled into town to negotiate with Clive, and now they want to show up for some sort of retribution. In the lifetime between our first encounter and now, our family has grown. We have loved, we have lost, and we damn sure have a lot more to lose now than we did then.

I bang the gavel down on the table. Sermon opens as Danza flips the door lock, securing the room.

"I'm not gonna beat around the bush, boys. We've lost too damn much," I begin. "What do we have on Paul Watson?" I look at Frisco, feeling the eyes of the younger members watching me, not knowing the name.

"Paul Shannon Watson, male, sixty-two years old. Currently resides in West Palm Beach, Florida. He previously served a nickel for weapons. He has one ex-wife, Jayne Wheatley, and one child resulting from the relationship. He patched to Fury MC in 1981, earned his diamond one-percenter patch in 1986. He has nine kills to his name for the club, and his current rank is president."

Danza stands, unable to remain still. "How does Fury tie into Rocky's crash? The cops tested the man; he was drunk. The beverage company even paid Dina out in a settlement."

"Fury runs transports with the company and holds a thirty percent stake in the company," Frisco answers, moving papers around in the file.

"Are you shittin' me?" I stand then pace the room right beside Danza. "We went soft. We let them sneak up on us. All this fucking time, they have been plan-nin', and we sat back and let them."

"How were we supposed to know?" Danza says, running his hands through his hair. "We were, like, fucking twenty when this shit started. Hell, we didn't know shit about a club back then. Think of all the mistakes we made. Shit, we landed our own asses in jail. Come on, Roundman, we had no way to know."

"Get Jayne and the kid here. It's time to find out what's gone on with Watson the last two decades. No better way than an ex-wife," I order.

Finishing the meeting, I dismiss the club, feeling the weight of it all bear down on my shoulders. We slipped up. I slipped up, and it cost my best friend and his wife their lives.

I won't slip up again. Paul Watson should have paid the price years ago for what happened with Clive. I let him off the hook.

Fool me once, shame on you; fool me twice, time to meet the reaper. And I'm going to be delivering his personal invitation to Hell.

TRUTH COMES OUT

FRISCO

As soon as Roundman issues the order, I head home to pack a bag.

Strolling inside my house, my mind is on what I need to pack. However, then I hear the sounds of Amy talking to herself and stop in my tracks.

"Breathe in and out." She inhales sharply and exhales loudly. "Gotta calm down, Amy. He's dead. The shop is gone. No one will get to you again."

Amy Mitchell, the woman who has lived with me

and worked with me for years now. She's a beautiful young woman with long brown hair, bright green eyes, and the hourglass figure that gets any red-blooded man hard. She's a beautiful person inside and out, but things between us are so beyond complicated.

She first showed up at the Hellions' compound with Felix Delatorre. He had threatened her family to get her to ship stuff for him, and then she ended up a bigger pawn in his game when Doll tried to help the woman.

When we set up the raid on Delatorre, Amy stepped in to help the Hellions. For that, I brought her back home. Since she's been here, we have had years of battling her anxiety and panic attacks.

She lives here with me. For about a year, I had to sleep with her in my arms in order for her to actually sleep. It's taken time to get her in her own room, but we are there now. At least I can rub one out privately when the urge hits me.

In a different lifetime, things may have worked out in another way for the two of us. But, long ago, I learned this life isn't for everyone. She's been through enough without me trying to remotely complicate anything else for either of us.

When I hit her bedroom door, I see her in some yoga pose, talking to herself. Her head is down, her ass is in the air, and she's trying to calm her breathing.

"Baby, you should stand up straight so all the blood ain't rushin' to your head."

She spreads her legs wide and peeks at me from between them. "Trying relaxing techniques. It's called Downward-Facing Dog."

"Looks to me like an invitation to take you from behind," I tell her honestly, fighting my dick from getting hard at the mere thought of fucking her.

"You big tease." She smiles at me, finally standing up and getting her spankable ass out of my face.

"Gotta take a trip for a while. The boys will be around if you need something. You can crash with Sass and Tank if you get too nervous. I'm sure she would love the help with Red."

Walking over to me wearing her workout pants and tank top that has her breasts pushing out of the top, thanks to her bra, she reaches up and pats my chest. Fire shoots through me like it does every time she touches me.

"Frisco, this ain't the first time you've had to leave me. I'm okay. I have good days and bad days, and I deal with it. You do what you gotta do."

"It's good to see you so strong."

She slides her hand up to my cheek, brushing my goatee with her thumb. "Thanks to you, I am. All thanks to you."

I wrap my arms around her and pull her close. "You always had it inside you. Be proud, Amy. You never let him break you."

She hugs me tightly before pulling slowly away. I can see the emotions she's trying to hold back in her eyes.

"Gotta get you packed and on the road," she says with a rasp in her voice before stepping away.

Going to my room, I head straight to the bathroom to shower.

The water is warm as I try to relax, but I can't. There is too much going on with the club, and this ride to Florida won't be easy.

Drying off, I simply wrap the towel around my waist before walking into my room where Amy is standing over my duffel bag, filling it on my bed.

I wrap my arms around her shoulders from behind, and she jumps at the contact before realizing it's me.

"You smell good," she says, continuing to pack.

"Soap works wonders."

She laughs, and I wish she did more of that.

She turns in my arms and wraps her own around

my waist, resting her head on my shoulder. "Gonna miss you, Frisco."

"Gonna miss you, Amy."

"Ride safe," she whispers before pulling back.

Tipping her chin to make her look at me, I lick my lips before I softly press mine to hers. She opens slightly, and I slip my tongue into her mouth. A moan escapes her as she explores my mouth. I feel her body tremble as she holds me tight, wanting more.

Groaning, I pull away, ending our kiss with a quick peck then trailing the hair of my goatee across her cheek. "Can't do this and then leave you."

She bites her bottom lip, looking contemplative. "Club comes first." The tone in which her words comes out isn't jealous nor malicious; it's more matter of fact. She simply accepts this part of my life.

I don't know how to take it.

I also don't have time to dwell on it since she happens to have my bag packed, and I really do need to get on the road.

She leaves me to my thoughts and to get dressed. Then, with a soft kiss good-bye, she sends me on my way.

———

D anza rides with me as we make the thirteen-hour trip to Jayne Wheatley's home where she lives with her daughter, Shannon Watson, Paul's only child. As soon as we cross into Georgia, we are on alert for any sign of Fury.

Pulling up to a non-descript residential neighborhood, I can't help wondering how the ol' lady to Paul Watson could live in such a cookie-cutter place. The house is cream stucco with Spanish-style roofing tiles. Palm trees sit at the corner of her driveway on each side.

We don't hide who we are when we ride straight up on our bikes into the cement driveway.

Nothing could prepare me for going up to Jayne Wheatley's front door. The doorbell chimes like any other. The door opens.

The woman in front of me is a shadow of someone I once knew. My heart stops, and questions fill my mind as to why she's here.

"Frisco," she whispers as I look deep into the hazel eyes I used to worship.

"No fuckin' way," Danza says over my shoulder.

I wish I could say time has done her good, but it hasn't. Her hair is brittle and sticking out wildly. Her face is wrinkled, but not in laugh lines like someone who lived a full life. Her lips have the marks of a woman who has smoked one too many cigarettes. The wrinkles from taking too many drags no longer fade away. And she's tan to the point of looking leathery.

Her eyes, though … They kill me.

The life is gone; the fight is gone. The woman who pushed so hard for me to choose her is a mess in front of me.

"Tilly …" I begin, wondering what the hell to say next.

"Mom?" I hear a teen voice calling out.

"Stay in your room. I'll be right there," Tilly orders back.

"We're looking for Jayne Wheatley," Danza says as I try to register why Matilda would be here of all places.

"You two need to go. Any other brothers you have with you need to turn around and hit 95 North and don't look back."

"Tilly," I say her name again.

She shakes her head at me.

"Fuck," Danza says, running his fingers through his hair crazily.

"I'm sorry, Frisco."

"Sorry?" I repeat as I try to click the pieces

together. "Loving me was part of a play with Watson? You're Jayne? You set me and my club up?"

She doesn't answer, but she looks to Danza. "I'm sorry for the time you lost."

His eyes grow wide.

"I'll fucking kill her myself," Danza says as we both start to mentally figure out what she's talking about.

Instead of continuing to stand on her front porch, I step into the doorway. Instinctively, she moves back as Danza follows me into her space.

"You better talk, and you better do it now if you want Shannon to even make it to tomorrow." I have never threatened a child before today, but this woman singlehandedly tried to rip me from my Hellions family.

Tears fill her eyes. "I guess it's time you know the truth."

"Truth? Do you even know the truth yourself?"

"Frisco, before you think of hurting her, you should know, she's yours."

Gripping both her shoulders, I pin her to the wall outside the house. "Bitch, don't you play games with me. You named her after Paul Shannon Watson. Don't think saying she's mine somehow will save her ass or yours."

"I deserve that and more. Kill me. I don't care, Frisco, but don't hurt her. She's the only thing I have good in my life." She pauses, and there is a heaviness in the air as my mind races. "I did love you, Richard. I wanted you to choose me, start over away from all of this, just you and me. I didn't want to be a pawn in Paul's game anymore. Once I got to know you, I really did care for you."

I don't know how to take her words. I don't know what to think about anything right now. And I don't have to, because Danza cuts in, his words pulling out my anger once more.

"Why'd you apologize to me? Say it, cunt. Say the words. Tell me how you cost me and my brother three years behind bars. Tell me how you did it, bitch," Danza says while I try to fight my urge to kill her and go see for myself if I really have a daughter or not.

She blows out a breath. "You deserve to hear me say it. I set you up. The day I kept Frisco home, I had been in touch with authorities. I set you up."

"You fuckin' cunt!" Danza roars. Even though he already knew what she would say, it's hitting him hard. "I lost years with my wife and child because of you! I fucking lost my mind because of wheels you set into motion."

The sound of Harleys pulling up gets our attention. I release Tilly to move to the hallway to see her daughter for myself before I deal with the members of Fury MC who are sure to be outside.

Pulling out our Glocks for protection, Danza and I proceed to clear out of the doorway and get farther into the house just as shots are fired.

I turn in time to see Tilly take a hit to the chest and fall. She doesn't scream, doesn't try to get out of the opening; she just takes what's coming. And inside, it kills a little piece of me.

"Get the kid," I say to Danza as I rush over to the woman I once cared for.

She's bleeding heavily as she takes another bullet to the leg and arm from the entryway. Getting low, I reach out and drag her toward me. Then I extend my arm out and fire wildly into the yard as I settle her head on my lap. The sound of someone cursing can be heard as I see Tilly has blood coming out of her mouth.

"Frisco, I'm sorry. I'm so sorry. She's yours," she chokes out as my jeans are saturated in her blood. "She's yours, Frisco. You gotta believe me; she is yours." The words strain to come out. "Promise me you'll keep her from Paul. He doesn't know. I just wanted a place to belong. He told me he'd give me that." She gasps for air as blood trickles from her nose and mouth. "He lied, Frisco. He gave me hell, not a home. Don't let Shannon go back to that."

The shots are still coming as Danza drags out a dark-haired teen girl behind him. Her eyes meet mine, and I swear I'm looking in a fucking mirror.

"Mom," she calls out from behind Danza, trying to see her mother, but the two of us are in her way.

"Shannon, my sweet, go with them when they say go. I love you, and I'm sorry." Tilly fights to keep her voice steady and not scare her daughter.

"If she's mine, I'll keep her from Paul," I give my word right as Tilly's eyes close and her head falls back.

"Gotta get the hell outta here. She goes with us," I tell Danza, getting to my feet.

The same second I spit out my orders, Shannon sees her mother and wails hysterically.

"Shannon's inside," I hear one of the assholes outside say. "Get out of here now! Prez won't want her hurt."

Well, thank fuck for that since she may very well be mine after all. I can't help wondering if Watson already sees that for himself, too. I'll kill him before he makes another play on my brothers, my club, and if she's mine, my daughter.

CHAPTER TWENTY

TAKE A STAND

ROUNDMAN

"Boomer and I aren't far behind you," I say to Frisco over the phone.

"We have a complication," he replies, and I can hear the stress in his voice.

"Spit it out," I snap as Boomer and I make our way to their location in the van.

"Shannon's mine," Frisco says without hesitation.

"How? Fuck! Does Watson know?"

"No. Jayne is Tilly; Tilly is Jayne, however you want to look at it."

"Get Shannon safe and then meet us at the rally point. Fury goes down tonight, and your girl comes home with her family."

It takes less than thirty minutes for Frisco to make the contact necessary to tuck Shannon away in a safe house with him. They need time together, and well, we have a club to take down. I don't know all the details of how he knows she's his, but just as Frisco has never questioned me, I will never question him.

Danza catches up to us, and in quick succession, we have eyes on Fury's compound. From our location in a house a mile away, Boomer gets busy creating the packages necessary to take out their entire facility.

In the meantime, I make a call that's been decades in the waiting.

"Only one person from North Carolina that'd be calling me," Watson answers. "Blaine Reklinger, took you long enough."

"Fuck you, Watson."

"Should've stayed out of this so long ago," he tells me. "Since ya didn't, I've had my own fun fucking with you when I've had the opportunity."

"I should have put a bullet in you years ago. I didn't, and for that, many others are going to suffer today. I'm taking your whole club out. Consider this the only warning you're gonna get."

"I'll be waiting for you, and this time, it's me who's gonna put your name on a single bullet and blow your brains out." He laughs. "Your reputation proceeds you. I know all about your one round rule, Roundman. To me, you're nothing but a joke." He disconnects before I can reply.

I want the whole motherfucking clubhouse up in flames.

It's not five minutes after our chat that the club begins to move, all of them in for a lockdown. Predictability in our lifestyle isn't smart. I would be wise to remember this for myself in the future.

This is a line we have never crossed before. Always, we keep women and children out of club problems. Today, I can't do that. Fury killed Rocky while he was on a family day with his wife. With no integrity to keep Marie safe, they set into motion the crash that left their daughter parentless. Well, whoever has aligned themselves with Fury dies today, and whether it was deserved or not will not be on my conscious.

Years ago, I let them go free, and for years, they have played with me and my family. Today, I take them all out. I won't have to look back again.

While they are busy in the hustle and bustle to get their members all accounted for and locked into one place, Boomer and our boys are using boats, robots, and their military skills to get small packages in place, surrounding the building and the open swamp around it. Fury was smart to set up away from society, but they also made themselves vulnerable. Their own cars are strapped with bombs they don't even know about.

———

Nine hours later, in the middle of the night, I watch Paul Watson come out from behind his gates. He stands out front, looking around, looking for us.

Coming out of the shadows, I confidently approach.

"You're one stupid motherfucker, Blaine Reklinger."

"You think?"

He gives me an arrogant smile. "You're a dead man."

"You think?"

"I know."

"Funny. I know some things, too. I know you thought you had Dia, yet you never even had a taste of that pussy. Let me tell you, it was fuckin' honey. I know you thought you had the upper hand on Clive. That shit bit you in the ass. I know your uncle got you out of Dodge and made you Fury's bitch to pay back the club for what you cost them. I know you're so far up my ass you let your woman suck my brother's cock, fuck him, and have his baby, all so you could send me to prison for a nickel that I didn't even serve the whole sentence of."

He says nothing, but the shock shows at my admission of Shannon's paternity.

"She may have your name, fucker, but she's got Hellions' blood runnin' in them veins. Don't worry, though; we'll teach her what family really is."

"Fuck you, Reklinger. You still don't know shit."

"I know you paid a guy to have some drinks and drive his truck into my brother's car, killing him and his wife. I know you got by with that one. But, cocky fuck like you, that wasn't good enough. You had to claim it, own it, and now you're gonna pay for it."

"It's done. And if you try a damn thing right now, you're a dead man. I got eyes, Reklinger."

I laugh in his face. "You should know you're not the first man to go after my club. You're not the first to come along and try to touch my family. You're not the first man who thought he had me by the balls. You should know I always win."

I pull out my revolver. I spin the clip.

"You should know each bullet in this gun has your name etched into it for every single time you've crossed me. You should know I'm gonna put each one of these in your chest. At the same time you're going down, so is your club."

I fire the first shot into his chest right as Boomer hits the switch, blowing up the front of the clubhouse.

Shots start to fire around us when I calmly send the next round into Paul, and Boomer sets the next explosion.

Each time I put a bullet in Watson, Boomer sends the club up into more of a fury of flames.

I fire the final shot and stand over the man who is now lying in a pool of his own blood while his empire burns behind us. The heat from the flames singes my eyebrows, but I stay still, watching him die. My skin is red from the temperature rising around me, but I remain steady, watching him die.

I feel no mercy. I feel no sympathy. I feel no satisfaction.

A good man died because of the man in front of me. A good man died with his wife, leaving behind their daughter because of the man in front of me. I lost family because of the actions of the man in front of me.

Tonight, he dies. Tonight, Fury MC dies. Tonight, the Hellions ride free from the chains of the past, free to go into the future.

I drop the gun over his body and walk off, not looking back. My club will clean it up. Nothing will come back on us.

I climb on my bike then hit 95 North without a single word to anyone.

Tonight, I ride free. Tonight, I am free from what started it all. Tonight, the Hellions ride as a club of our own making, and never again will one person from Fury touch my family.

The Hellions have always and will always be about protecting our own at all costs.

CHAPTER

TWENTY ONE

A LESSON IN FAMILY

FRISCO

W hat the hell do I do now? I have a daughter. I have an eighteen-year-old daughter who has no clue who I am and just watched her mother die at the hands of the men she thought were her father's men. Shit was complicated before, but now, I don't even know if there is a word to describe the mess I'm in.

Having Shannon climb on my bike behind me felt strange. There have only ever been two women on my bike: Tilly, or Jayne—I need to sort out who she really was—and Amy. With Tilly, she always held on tightly, but in a stiff way, never letting loose. Amy went from timid and shaking to now climbing on and feeling the world around her as we ride.

I feel Shannon's body tremble as she tries not to hold me. My daughter's hands barely touch my waist as I pull off to get her to the safe house.

The place belongs to an old buddy I made long before the Hellions. He builds racing bikes for the drag strip. He has a small room over his bike shop we can crash in for a bit and sort out what's what before I take her home to North Carolina.

I laugh to myself as I pull into his drive, thinking of the boy who never had a place to call home, yet here I am, thinking about taking my own child to the place I now call home. What a twisted road life has taken me on.

Shannon is visibly shaking as we dismount. I see the tear streaks down her face. The good inside me wants to comfort her. The man who has been fucked over one too many times wants to hold on to the hope that she's not mine, even as my heart screams she is.

"Let's get inside, and then we'll sort shit," I spit the words out then try to stop myself from cussing.

I shake my head and make my way upstairs,

sending a text to Mikey as I go so he knows who's here and why I'm in his spot.

Lifting the third rail of the porch, I find the hidden key and get us in.

The space is a simple loft with a kitchenette, a queen bed, and a sofa. There isn't much in the way of privacy with a tri-fold screen being the only thing to separate the toilet and shower from the rest of the space. Beggars can't be choosers. I'm just thankful to have a place I know we will be safe for a little while until I can sort things with Shannon and get back on the road.

The ping of my phone gives me the info that Fury has been handled.

Guilt hits me like a punch to the nuts. Will Shannon hate me for what my club has done? The only man she's ever known as her father is dead, and it's by my brothers' hands.

He had it coming. Truth be told, if we could bring him back to life for each of us to have a turn at killing him over and over, he really deserved it. We aren't a club to typically take down an entire facility. Women and children are normally protected, but with Fury, they used a woman against us when Paul sent Tilly— well, Jayne—to seduce me and tear us apart from the inside out.

"Frisco?" Shannon's voice comes out soft.

"Yeah?" I look at her then have to look away because her eyes are my own.

"Mom"—she pauses—"well, she didn't mean to do it."

"What do you know?"

Moving to the couch, she sits as if the weight of carrying herself is too much.

My stomach twists as I think of the pain and loss she's enduring right now.

"More than I should," she gives me honestly. "Looking at you, it's obvious my dad is not my dad. Thinking about it now, he had a plan for me, too. Things he said over the years … He was buying time, and then he was going to show me to you. He would always tell Mom the day would come when he would proudly have me on display like his trophy from the Hellions."

Paul Watson thought my daughter was some prize trophy to hold over my club instead of the beautiful young woman she is. I fight the urge to punch something.

"I know it's not easy, but can you tell me more?" I ask.

"I know my mom was with him when she was young. She was, like, fourteen-ish when she met him.

He was down here on vacation, visiting his uncle Cheeks, who was in Fury. He went back to North Carolina because that's where he lived. Then Mom said he suddenly lived here and was trying to patch into the club. She said she thought the life on the edge was exciting and fell hopelessly in love with him. Then Paul Watson was no more, and in his place was 'Victory,' or Vic, as the guys in the club called him. He was consumed by some club called the Hellions, which I see now are you guys."

"Did your mom tell you about us?"

She shakes her head. "Not your club, but you. I know about you. Vic thought you were his way in. Mom said she met you, and the more she fought to do what he wanted her to do, the more she found herself loving you." Tears fall down her face. "I know you won't believe me, but I don't think my mom intended to hurt you like she did. But if you knew Vic, you would know she had to do what he wanted."

I pace the room, unable to speak.

"Mom said she spent a few years in North Carolina with you. In fact, she always promised me she would take me there one day so I could see the peaceful, quiet areas without all the hustle and bustle. She said she reached a point where she was broken up inside, and you walked away for her to be free.

Knowing she couldn't stay in the area and see you move on, she came back to Florida."

At her pause, I look into her eyes and see fear. "Go on," I encourage. "What's got you upset?"

"She said she first came back to Florida because it was home, but she tried to break up with my dad—I mean Vic," she stumbles. "He wouldn't have any part of it, even though he was never faithful to Mom. I've seen more whores in and out of his room than I thought one man could handle." She blows out a breath. "It was me. She was pregnant with me. She always told me how hard she found it to give me a different life. For me, she married him. She would have stayed, but he got tired of her spells."

"Spells?" I ask, hating reliving my daughter's childhood like this.

"Depression. The doctor said it was depression. Mom said it was heartbreak and guilt because she deserved the pain. Either way, she had spells where she would cut herself, like, all over and just lie there, bleeding. She never cut deep enough to bleed out, like suicide, but enough to hurt herself."

Immediately, I remember back to the last day on my bed when she cut herself and then me.

"I'm sorry you went through all that, Shannon."

"She had a good heart, Frisco. She just didn't

know how to handle things. Vic is a mean bastard of a man. She made the best of things." Her dark eyes look up and meet mine. "Please don't hate her."

What the hell do I say to that?

I shake my head as a battle wages on inside my heart. Tilly fucked me in every way imaginable, and now my daughter—our daughter—wants me not to hate the woman who tried to take it all from me.

"Frisco, she really did care about you. She was in a mess that was bigger than you or I could ever understand. I'll go with you. I'll go to North Carolina. Just please don't hate my mom. She could have left me in that club with the whores, but she didn't. She had her spells, but never when I was around, and she always took care of me. She was a good mom. I can't go with you, knowing you hate her when she's all I ever had."

Thinking back to my own childhood and the many times I lay on concrete beside my mom just so she wouldn't be alone, I understand what Shannon feels.

"I don't hate your mom. In fact, I respect your loyalty."

She twists her hands nervously. "What's going to happen to me?"

"I'm going to take you home with me. You're going to learn what I learned from the Hellions.

Family isn't always blood. Our club isn't like Fury, Shannon. You're safe, and you're family."

"I hope what you say is true."

"You'll see. I promise you'll see the Hellions are family, and they'll take you as you are. They did me. You will get a firsthand lesson in family with my club." I give her a smile, thinking about the chance I have to let my daughter experience the best kind of family there is—the Hellions family.

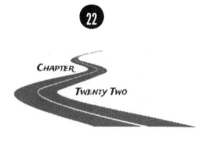

HOLDING ON

DANZA

"You okay, brother?" I look at Roundman and see the tired look in his eyes.

"Times are changing."

"What's that mean?"

He leans back in his office chair for a beat. It's just me and him today. Jenna, Ruby's wife, is in the customer area, but she can't hear us and knows better than to disturb us.

Standing, Roundman goes to one of the filing

cabinets that line the wall of his office. Grabbing a folder, he moves to his safe then takes out the bullet he put inside years ago. Then he rolls the metal casing in his fingers and smiles.

"There was a time when I wanted to use this."

I laugh. "On Tripp?"

"It's got his name on it," he gives me back sarcastically.

"He's a good man. Damn good club prez," I back up my Catawba Hellions' charter and Roundman's son-in-law.

"He is. I know you wanted to fuck shit up for Tank before he fixed himself and made things right with Sass."

"Yeah," I reply honestly. "He's straight now. Tank's a better man to my daughter than I was to her momma years ago."

Roundman studies me. "You still feeling the guilt, Danza? Come on, we were young. You fucked up, you owned it, and you've spent years making that shit right with Mary Alice."

"I'll spend a lifetime, and it still won't be enough."

"I had a lifetime of Dia's love, and it wasn't enough."

I raise an eyebrow at my longtime friend. "You ever think of moving on?"

"Nope. Love like that doesn't come twice."

"Then what's the change you're talking about?"

He tosses the folder onto his desk and gets comfortable in his chair. "Club business, shop business, mini storage business."

I gesture with my hand for him to go on.

"Ain't getting' any younger. Need to know what parts you want, Danza."

"You steppin' down?"

He shakes his head. "Not yet, but we need to think of the long-term and who will be where." He slides a piece of paper over to me. "That's from my lawyer, giving you the garage. If Tripp and Doll move home, they'll have the storage. As for the club, when the time comes, I can pass the gavel to you or take it to a vote for Tripp. You tell me, brother; what do you feel?"

I blow out a breath. That's a loaded question.

"I feel like you just dropped the world on me. I feel like there is more going on than you are telling me."

"Frisco has a whole new family situation and eighteen years of life to catch up on. You're my VP, and you've always had my back. I want what you want when the time comes that I'm not wearing this prez patch anymore." He rubs his goatee. "No need to answer right now, but I need you to think on it."

"I don't want to wear your patch, Roundman. It's yours and always has been. If you step down, I step down, too." Plain and simple, just as it should be.

"We'll talk more on it soon," he says right as his desk phone rings for a transport.

Well, at least I have time to get used to the idea.

———

As I walk in the house Mary Alice and I have shared for so long, it's quiet. Too quiet. My wife is always in the kitchen or cleaning something. She doesn't sit still, doesn't nap, and she doesn't sit quietly in a room somewhere, contemplating life.

Only, when I go into our bedroom. that's what she's doing. With her wedding band rolling between her fingers, she sits silently on our bed.

"Mary Alice," I greet, entering the space.

She looks up at me, her eyes swollen and tears streaming down her face.

Rushing to her, I drop to my knees at her side. "What's wrong? Is it Sass? Red?" I ask as worry fills me for our daughter and grandson. "That fucker Nick didn't come around, did he? I'll handle it, Mary Alice."

"Will you handle you?" she asks me in a whisper.

"Huh?"

"All these years, Rhett, I've never known any love but yours."

"Where are you going with this?"

"You are the only man I've ever given my heart, my body, and my life to."

Guilt immediately eats at me. "Mary Alice, it's only you."

"Now, yes, it is." She laughs sarcastically. "You know, the first time you stepped out, Dia said, Mary Alice, y'all were young. He's a man; he just needed to try something different. We even laughed about how you were better in bed after the barfly taught you a thing or two. I found a way to get passed it. Then you went to jail.

"For three years, Rhett, I stood by and raised our daughter, made sure you had what you needed, visited, and I held you down."

"I never said you didn't."

She reaches out and runs her fingers over my cheek and lips. I kiss her palm softly. God, don't let this be the end.

"Our daughter turned her back on everything we

taught her because of me, Rhett. She couldn't stand the woman I had become, the things I stood by and allowed for the sake of the club and the sake of being your ol' lady. My own daughter was ashamed of the woman she thought I was."

"She doesn't feel that way now. She understands, Mary Alice. Everyone in the club understands. I fucked up, baby. I fucked up beyond a fuck up. I ruined what we had, not you. I promised you, when I came home from jail. After we lost Rocky and Marie, I promised you. I straightened my shit out, no more barflies, no more leaving you behind. I calculated the risks, and baby, you gotta know I've been faithful."

"It's not about you, Rhett. It's not about Danza's role in the Hellions. Don't you see it's about me?"

"Where is this coming from? Fuck, where is it heading?"

She shakes her head, and panic fills her eyes. "I don't know, Rhett. I don't know anymore. I didn't just marry you; I married into the Hellions. We're family. The club has always supported me when you failed to do so. When Ruby and Vida took their time apart, the club came together not only for him, but her and their kids. When Boomer and Pam rolled into town, we all took her back, helping her mom and kids even though they were from the Catawba chapter. Hellions are family regardless of their chapter.

"Things are changing. The time is coming when Dia and I were supposed to sit back and watch our girls fill our shoes."

I nod as dread consumes me.

"She's not here to do it with me. I miss my friend. I miss the life I thought we would have. Marie is gone. Rocky, too. We have loved, Rhett. We have lost. Where does the ride go now?"

"Wherever we let it take us, baby. It goes wherever we let it lead us. But, Mary Alice, please tell me we do it together."

She tilts her head to the side, studying me. "Why?"

"Why?" I choke out. "Because we have loved; we have lost; we have broken; and dammit, we've rebuilt. We are going into the prime of our lives, and there isn't a single soul I want to share that with but you. I was young. I was dumb. But, baby, I did everything I could to keep you safe, build a life for us together, and keep us together. I made mistakes along the way, and that's on me, not you, but I've changed, and you know it. Let me have the opportunity to spend the rest of our days giving you everything I should have been giving you from the start."

She shakes her head. "I made a fool of myself by standing by you. I've been your doormat—come in, wipe your feet off, take off a load, find your release, and walk right back over me on your way out. I allowed it."

Climbing onto the bed over her, I bring my eyes level with hers. "Don't. Please, Mary Alice, don't you do it."

"I love you, Rhett, but where did it all go so wrong? Why did I let it all slide? Dia told me I should have kicked your ass more often. I didn't. Blaine has never let himself love again. I can't say that, if it had been me and not Dia, you would have given me the same loyalty."

"Maybe there was a time I wouldn't have. I can't go back in time and change things, Mary Alice. I can tell you that, for years, I have been loyal, loving, faithful, and for as many days as you give me, I'll give you my everything. I can tell you that, if tomorrow were to come and this was no more, I would never have a love like we share again. You are it for me, Mary Alice, and I took that for granted once, but I won't do it again."

With shaking hands, she cups my face and pulls me to her, kissing me softly. I taste the salt of her tears, and the need to be one with her consumes me as I deepen our kiss.

Breaking away, I drop my head to her neck. "I'm sorry I hurt you. I'm sorry I took you for granted. I'm sorry for all the pain between us."

I kiss her neck before I roll us to our sides and kiss her lips again. Wrapping her leg around me, I let my hand tease her through her cloth pants and panties.

"I love you, Mary Alice. I promise you it's only ever been you in my heart. You own me, baby. I promise you my loyalty." I kiss her again as she tightens her arms around me.

Slowly, tenderly, I give my wife what I should have given her years before as I make love to her body. I give her my heart, my soul, and my body. I give her every part of me, knowing without a shadow of a doubt, for me and her, this is our forever ride together in life. We could have lost it all, should have lost it all, but in the end, she loved me through everything, and I'll love her until the end of time.

CHAPTER
TWENTY THREE

COULDN'T BE PROUDER

ROUNDMAN

I ring the doorbell at the same time I hear something crash to the floor.

Pulling the gun from my back, I ready myself as I twist the doorknob, only to find it unlocked.

Entering the space, I find my precious Doll on the floor naked. Her husband Tripp is on top of her with her legs around his shoulders just as he thrusts hard, groaning her name.

"Fucking shit, Tripp. I should shoot your naked ass."

"Daddy!" Doll squeals, pulling her legs down and her husband down to cover herself. "What the hell are you doing here?"

I turn my head toward the kitchen. "Surprise." I don't hide my sarcasm. "I'll go make myself a snack. You two better have made me a granddaughter during your little tryst."

"Nothing little about me or about how I fuck my wife," Tripp gives back smartly.

"Shoulda put that fuckin' bullet in you years ago."

I go into the kitchen to get a snack, listening to my daughter scramble around before I feel her two small arms come around and hug me from behind. Her blonde hair is sticking out everywhere just like her mom's used to.

I reach behind me and give her a squeeze.

"Be right back. Tripp will need his T-shirt back, and I'm sure you want me to not remind you of what we were doing."

I laugh. Then on a sigh, I watch as she scurries away to get dressed.

"You'll always be my little girl, Doll," I whisper to the space around me.

It's not long before the two of them are in front of me again. Tripp reaches out, and we exchange the normal handshake, half-hug, and back slap before I give my daughter a proper hug now that she's wearing her own clothes again.

"Where are the boys?" Tripp asks, looking for the rest of the club.

"In Haywood's Landing."

"You came alone?" My daughter questions with concern.

"Prez doesn't need to ride alone," Tripp reminds me of something I know very well.

"I didn't come here for Hellions' business. I came here to see my daughter." With my explanation out, I lift the envelope from my back pocket. "You were too young when your mother passed on to have this. The time has come, Delilah, that you get another piece of her."

Putting the envelope to my lips, I inhale, barely able to smell her perfume as I let go of the last thing I've held on to for our daughter. The envelope is wrinkled and faded from years of being tucked away. However, Claudia's script is still bold and full of the love she put into it when she wrote the letter.

Sitting down at her dining room table, my precious Doll breaks the seal that was last touched by her mother's lips. On a sigh and with tears already filling her eyes, she reads the letter barely above a whisper as her voice cracks with emotions.

My dearest Doll, Delilah,

Oh, baby girl, how I wished for you, prayed for you, and loved having you. If you're reading this, then the cancer won, and my precious, I'm so sorry to leave you. Please know I do so with the knowledge that you have a family with the Hellions and a father who will give his own life before he lets any harm ever come to a single blonde hair on your head.

The time will come in your life when things will shift. It's called change, and baby, we all have to go through it. Mary Alice will give this letter to your dad so that he can determine when the time is right for you to have this piece of me, this piece of our life, and this piece of advice for your future.

I hope that, as you read this, you have come to terms with the decisions your dad and I made many years ago about having a club life. Although exhilarating at times, the Hellions didn't come to be because of some need for a thrill ride, Doll. No matter what direction life takes the club, please go back to the roots of it all and remember it's family, loyalty, and love above all else.

Your father took a stand for what he believed in many years ago, and the Hellions formed out of necessity to keep those closest to him safe. Times weren't always easy, and my precious, as much as I want your life to be simple and smooth, you, too, will have to ride through the rough patches as they come.

We could have walked away from the club many times, and maybe we should have—I don't know. What I do know is, if you're reading this, the club stands firm. Understand that no matter what the dangers, the risks, and the losses we faced, the club continues out of love and loyalty. Ride until we die.

Doll, the Hellions are your family, your safe place, and your father will stand strong until the time comes that he feels it's right to pass along what it means to be a leader.

Blaine is a man of great pride. Doll, you have to know he's proudest of you. In saying this, you will also need to know that, when the time comes, it will be out of pride that things come to a head, and your dad will make decisions, very hard decisions. And I can't predict the future, my precious, but I know he does so with your best interest at heart.

I write you this letter so you understand you are a Hellion through and through. The love Blaine and I have for you, the club also has for you.

My time with you is all too short, my Delilah, but please know that I leave you my heart.

My heart is full of love for your dad, you, our

club, and the future. My heart is full of loyalty to those who have never let me down.

My heart is full of hope for you, my daughter. I hope that you find the love of a man who is strong, a man who will not back down in the tough times yet love you tenderly each and every night. My hope for you is a future where you can watch your man take his place in something he believes in and ride until you die. Doll, you stand with him as he does so. It won't be easy, but my girl, you have my strength; you can stand strong against every curve in life's road.

My hope for you is to have children just as wonderful as you are who can give you back the love you gave to your dad and me.

My hope for you, my dearest Doll, is that no matter what, you know yourself inside and out. You know where you came from, what you believe in, and that, when life gives you choices on which path to take, you ride strong on the path least taken.

Be fearless, my Delilah, love hard, and remember where you came from.

I'm always with you, watching over you. Carry my heart with you, carry my love through you, and ride every curve with pride and loyalty.

Loving you through eternity,

Mom

Tears fall down my daughter's face as she finishes the letter, and I fight back my own emotions.

"What does this mean?"

"You are so much like your mom, Doll."

She gives me a fierce grin. "We all know that, Dad. What's going on here?"

"Nothing yet, but times are changing, and I need you to know where you came from." I look at Tripp. "I need you both to know the Hellions were born out of necessity, but we ride on out of love and loyalty. This is your family."

"Are you stepping down?" Tripp gives me his honest thoughts like always.

"Talon, when the time comes for my final ride, you will know. Things are changing, and the future path isn't always so clear, so when I know, you'll know, son."

Doll jumps up with tears coming down her face. She buries her head against my chest as she holds me close.

I look over her at her man. "Tripp, I respect you, and I believe in you. When the time comes, you will have my vote. That's something the two of you need to consider. For now, let's go for a ride as a family."

"BW is with Rex and Lux, so let me grab my helmet," Doll says, stepping away.

"You sure about this, Roundman?" Tripp asks out of earshot from Doll.

"Not yet, but a man's gotta know when it's time to take a different path."

Less than five minutes later, I'm on my bike with my daughter holding on to her husband as he rides beside me. Slowing, I let Tripp take the lead in front of me.

I feel the memories of Claudia's hands roaming my chest while we rode. I feel her body behind me, her legs against my own, and her hair whipping around, slapping me in the face. I feel the wind squeeze me as I look ahead to see my daughter in front of me, riding free.

"*Love you for eternity, Blaine,*" Claudia whispers in my mind.

Riding free, I press on, knowing Claudia will always have my heart, and the future we wished for is right in front of me.

PART FOUR INTRODUCTION

PART FOUR

OUT OF LEGACY...
IT SURVIVES

I've loved, and I've lost. I've conquered, I've killed, and I've barely survived. Everything has been from one up to the next down, but I've never done it without my woman in my heart and my brothers at my side.

The Hellions will always ride together with life, love, and the freedom of the road to soothe everything that burdens the soul. Ride until I die, love with all I have until I have no more, and damn sure remember family is a never ending circle of love and loyalty that lasts a lifetime when you get it right.

~Roundman~

ROUNDMAN

The gray stone is damp with morning dew. The flowers droop in the weight of the atmosphere.

Claudia Reklinger
Devoted wife and mother

I trace the letters as I talk to the air around me. "My best friend, my life, my wife, my love, ride until I die. Baby, it's you."

Squatting in front of the tombstone, I pinch the bridge of my nose, fighting back emotions. I'm a motherfucking Hellion, yet the minute I let my mind go back to what I once had, I turn to mush.

"Doll, she's bringing BW to visit. God, he's a handful. Fearless, baby, fucking fearless. He has your hair and Tripp's eyes. Doll hasn't gotten it cut yet, so it frames his chubby face with your blonde curls. He runs our girl ragged. Makes me think of you when Doll was little."

I smile, thinking back to our tiny girl coming home, all bundled in red because Dia hated pink. My two girls were inseparable. Dia was an amazing mother.

Then the cancer came. Then the cancer won.

"Our time together was cut too short." Over twenty years later, I want to break shit just thinking about it.

It took time—years to be honest—for me to get the shop and give my girl my last name. We were young and thought we could rule the world. And in the end, I did my best to give that to her. We may not have conquered cancer, but we had the Hellions, and Haywood's Landing was ours.

"Family isn't always blood. We taught our daughter that. With Tripp having his club, being with Shooter and his family, along with Rex and his ol' lady, our girl understands family isn't always blood."

I blow out a breath. "Damn, Dia, she's beautiful. Our Doll is all grown up. She's as fierce as you and loyal. We should have made it her middle name. It's a part of who she is."

I close my eyes and breathe deeply. "You once told me it takes a club. You were right. It has taken a club to get us all this far. I wish you were here to see it, baby. Time's comin', Dia. The time for change is here. The legacy of the Hellions needs to be passed on."

I lay the flowers against the cement tombstone. "I need you to guide me. Is our baby girl ready to be an ol' lady to the entire club, not just one charter? Tripp can handle it, even if he doesn't realize it yet. Danza even said so. Getting old isn't an easy thing to face."

On a sigh, I touch my fingers to my lips then press them to the D on the stone. "Love you, Dia." In my mind, I can still hear her voice, *"Love you always, Blaine."*

Climbing on my bike, I ride out. I hit the open road and don't look back.

After I stop for gas, I keep riding until I find myself at the shack in Deals Gap, North Carolina.

As the sun sets, I make the start of the Dragon's Tail ride. For a moment, I swear I can feel her arms around me and her hair whipping against my face. I take each curve leisurely as I allow my mind to go back in time. All the years I took this ride with my wife behind me flash through like a movie playing on repeat. The many times I took this ride to patch another man into the club I created.

One by one, each of us has made this same ride before calling ourselves a true brother to the Hellions MC. Today, I take this ride before I go see my daughter and her man to pass on the legacy to the next generation.

From beginning to end, this is how the Hellions ride, and this is how the legacy will survive. With a twist of my throttle, I ride on, knowing what's to come with complete clarity for the first time in a long time.

THE END...

Until the next ride.

Final Ride will be the last book in the Hellions Ride series.

ABOUT THE AUTHOR

USA Today and Wall Street Journal bestselling author Chelsea Camaron is a small-town Carolina girl with a big imagination. She's a wife and mom, chasing her dreams. She writes contemporary romance, romantic suspense, and romance thrillers. She loves to write about blue-collar men who have real problems with a fictional twist. From mechanics, bikers, oil riggers, smokejumpers, bar owners, and beyond she loves a strong hero who works hard and plays harder.

Chelsea can be found on social media at:

Facebook: www.facebook.com/authorchelseacamaron

Twitter: @chelseacamaron

Instagram: @chelseacamaron

Website: www.authorchelseacamaron.com

Email chelseacamaron@gmail.com

Join Chelsea's reader group here: http://bit.ly/2BzvTa4

ALSO BY CHELSEA CAMARON

Love and Repair Series:

Crash and Burn

Restore My Heart

Salvaged

Full Throttle

Beyond Repair

Stalled

Box Set Available

Hellions Ride Series:

One Ride

Forever Ride

Merciless Ride

Eternal Ride

Innocent Ride

Simple Ride

Heated Ride

Ride with Me (Hellions MC and Ravage MC Duel with

Ryan Michele)

Originals Ride

Final Ride

Hellions Ride On Series:

Hellions Ride On Prequel

Born to It

Bastard in It

Bleed for It

Breathe for It

Bold from It

Broken by It

Brazen being It

Better as It

Blue Collar Bad Boys Series:

Maverick

Heath

Lance

Wendol

Reese

Devil's Due MC Series:

Serving My Soldier

Crossover

In The Red

Below The Line

Close The Tab

Day of Reckoning

Paid in Full

Bottom Line

Almanza Crime Family Duet

Cartel Bitch

Cartel Queen

Romantic Thriller Series:

Stay

Seeking Solace: Angelina's Restoration

Reclaiming Me: Fallyn's Revenge

Bad Boys of the Road Series:

Mother Trucker

Panty Snatcher

Azzhat

Santa, Bring Me a Biker!

Santa, Bring Me a Baby!

Stand Alone Reads:

Romance – Moments in Time Anthology

Shenanigans (Currently found in the Beer Goggles
Anthology

<u>She is …</u>

The following series are co-written

The Fire Inside Series:

(co-written by Theresa Marguerite Hewitt)

<u>Kale</u>

Regulators MC Series:

(co-written by Jessie Lane)

<u>Ice</u>

<u>Hammer</u>

<u>Coal</u>

Summer of Sin Series:

(co-written with Ripp Baker, Daryl Banner, Angelica

Chase, MJ Fields, MX King)

Original Sin

Caldwell Brothers Series:

(co-written by USA Today Bestselling Author MJ Fields)

Hendrix

Morrison

Jagger

Stand Alone Romance:

(co-written with USA Today Bestselling Author MJ Fields)

Visibly Broken

Use Me

Ruthless Rebels MC Series:

(co-written with Ryan Michele)

Shamed

Scorned

Scarred

Schooled

Box Set Available

Power Chain Series:

(co-written with Ryan Michele)

<u>Power Chain FREE eBook</u>

<u>PowerHouse</u>

<u>Power Player</u>

<u>Powerless</u>

OverPowered

FINAL RIDE

FINAL RIDE
Hellions Ride: Book 9

E verything I have never had is right in front of me. Family, it's mine for the taking. For the first time in my life, I found stability in the Hellions MC. From the ground up, I've been loyal to my brothers.

Now the time has come when I may have to choose between the family I've never known or the club I've built and given my all to.

Richard 'Frisco' Billings is the California kid who rode into Haywood's Landing when the Hellions were needing an extra man. As an original, he's been with the club from day one. After growing up with no real place to call home, he's found solid ground.

All of it crashed around him when secrets were revealed, and he found out he missed all the formative years with his daughter being raised in an enemy's club.

Amy Mitchell was lost her whole life until she was found by the Hellions MC in a bad situation with Felix Delatorre. She spent years with the club, rebuilding her life and finding a place where she could belong.

When a new young woman comes into the home she has with Frisco, will she still fit into his world? Will Frisco find a way to make everything fit together? Will this be his final ride with the Hellions as life takes him down a different road?

Catch up with all your favorite couples as every secret finds its way out of the dark and new things are revealed, changing the club forever. This is the final ride for the Hellions MC as we know it.

IN THE RED EXCERPT

The event that shook one small town to its core was never solved. The domino effect of one person's crime going unpunished is beyond measure.

He's no saint.

Dover 'Collector' Ragnes rides with only five brothers at his back. Nomads with no place to call home, they never stay in one place too long. Together, they are the Devil's Due MC, and their only purpose is to serve justice their way for unsolved crimes everywhere they go.

She's not afraid to call herself a sinner.

Emerson Flint still remembers the loss of her elementary school best friend. She is all grown up, but the memories still haunt her of the missing girl. Surrounding herself with men at the tattoo shop, she never questions her safety. Her life is her art. Her canvas is the skin of others.

However, danger is at her door.

Will Dover overcome the history he shares with Emerson in time? Will Emerson lead him to the retribution he has always sought?

Love, hate, anger, and passion collide as the time comes, and the devil demands his due.

PROLOGUE

I hang my head and sit in silence. The television blares as strangers move about our house. Some of them are trying to put together a search party, and others are here with food and attempts to comfort. I want them all to go away. I want to scream or break something. I want them all to stop looking at me like I should be beaten within an inch of my life then allowed to heal, only to get beaten again. Do I deserve that?

Hell yes, I do, and more.

There is no reprieve from the hell we are in. I would sell my soul to the Devil himself if I could turn back time. Only, I can't.

The reporter's voice breaks through all of the clamor.

"In local news tonight, a nine-year-old girl is missing, and authorities are asking for your help. Raleigh Ragnes was last seen by her seventeen-year-old brother. According to her parents, her brother was watching her afterschool when the child wandered outside and down the street on her pink and white bicycle with streamers on the handlebars.

"She was last known to have her brown hair braided with a yellow ribbon tied at the bottom. She was in a yellow shirt and a black denim dress that went to her knees. She wore white Keds with two different color laces; one is pink, and one is purple.

"There is a reward offered for any information leading to the successful return of Raleigh to her home. Any information is appreciated and can be given by calling the local sheriff's department."

The television seems to screech on and on with other reports as if our world hasn't just crumbled. My mom's sobs only grow louder.

God, I'm an ass. Raleigh was whining all afternoon about going to Emerson's house. Those two are practically inseparable. She had made the trip numerous times to the Flint's home at the end of the cul-de-sac, so I didn't think twice about her leaving.

Gretchen was here, locked in my room with me. My hand was just making it down her pants when I yelled at Raleigh through the door to just go, not wanting the distraction. My mind was only occupied with getting into Gretchen's pants.

Only, while I was making my way to home base, my little sister never made it to her friend's house. None of us knew until dinner time arrived and my sister never came home. The phone call to Emerson's sent us all into a tailspin.

While other families watch the eleven o'clock news to simply be informed, for my family, my little sister is the news.

~Three weeks later ~

The television screeches once again. I thought the world had crumbled before, but now it's crushed and beyond repair. The reporter's tone is not any different than if they were giving the local weather as the words they speak crash through my ears.

"In local news tonight, the body of nine-year-old Raleigh Ragnes was found in a culvert pipe under Old Mill Road. Police are asking for anyone with any information to please come forward. The case is being treated as an open homicide."

In the matter of a month, my sister went from an innocent little girl to a case number, and in time, she will be nothing more than a file in a box. Everyone else may have called it cold and left it unsolved, but that's not who I am.

The domino effect of one person's crime going unpunished is beyond measure.

DOVER

*G*iving up is not an option for me ... It never has been.

"There's a time and a place to die, brother," I say, scooping Trapper's drunk ass up off the dirty floor of the bar with both my hands under his armpits. "This ain't it."

It's a hole in the wall joint, the kind we find in small towns everywhere. It's a step above a shack on the outside, and the inside isn't much better: one open room, linoleum floor from the eighties. The bar runs the length of the space with a pair of saloon-style swinging doors closing off the stock room. We have gotten shit-faced in nicer, and we have spent more than our fair share of time in worse.

At the end of a long ride, a cold beer is a cold

beer. Really, it doesn't matter to us where it's served as long as it has been on ice and is in a bottle.

"I'm nowhere near dying," he slurs, winking at the girl he has had on his lap for the last hour. She's another no name come guzzler in a slew of many we find throughout every city, town, and stop we make. "In fact, I'm not far from showing sweet thing here a little piece of heaven."

"Trapper." Judge, the calmest of us all, gets in his face. "She rode herself to oblivion until you fell off the stool. She's done got hers, man. Time to get you outta here so you can have some quality time huggin' Johnny tonight."

We all laugh as Trapper tries to shake me off. "Fuck all y'all. That pussy is mine tonight."

"Shithead, sober up. She's off to the bathroom to snort another line, and she won't be coming back for another ride on your thigh. Time to go, brother," Rowdy says sternly.

Trapper turns to the redheaded, six-foot, six-inch man of muscle and gives him a shit-eating grin. "Aw, Rowdy, are you gonna be my sober sister tonight?"

I wrap my arm around Trapper, pulling him into a tight hold. "Shut your mouth now!"

He holds up his hands in surrender, and we make our way out of the bar.

Another night, another dive. Tomorrow is a new day and a new ride.

Currently, we are in Leed, Alabama for a stop off. The green of the trees, the rough patches of the road —it all does nothing to bring any of us out of the haunting darkness we each carry.

We're nomads—no place to call home, and that's how we like it. The six of us have been a club of our own creation for almost two years now. We all have a story to tell. We all have a reason we do what we do. None of us are noble or honorable. We strike in the most unlikely of places and times, all based on our own brand of rules and systems.

Fuck the government. Fuck their laws. And damn sure fuck the judicial system.

Once your name is tainted, no matter how good you are, you will never be clean in the eyes of society. I'm walking, talking, can't sleep at night proof of it. Well, good fucking deal. I have learned society's version of clean is everything I don't ever want to be.

The scum that blends into our communities and with our children, the cons that can run a game, they think they are untouchable. The number of crimes outnumber the crime fighters. The lines between law abiding and law breaking blur every day inside every precinct. I know because I carried the badge and thought I could be a change in the world. Then I found out everything is just as corrupt for the people upholding the law as those breaking it.

Day in and day out, watching cops run free who deserve to be behind bars more than the criminals they put away takes its toll. Everyone has a line in the sand, and once they cross it, they don't turn back. I found mine, and I found the brotherhood in the Devil's Due MC. Six guys who have all seen our own fair share of corruption in the justice system. Six guys who don't give a fuck about the consequences.

Well, that's where me and my boys ride in. No one's above the devil getting his due. We are happy to serve up our own kind of punishments that most certainly fit the crimes committed, and we don't bother with the current legal system's view of justice served.

We're wayward souls, damaged men, who have nothing more than vengeance on our minds.

"Fucking bitch, she got my pants wet," Trapper says, just realizing she really did get off on his thigh and left him behind. "You see this shit?" He points at his leg.

Trapper mad is good. He will become focused rather than let the alcohol keep him in a haze. He could use some time to dry up. He's sharp. His attention to detail saves our asses in city after city. However, things get too close to home when we ride to the deep south like this, and he can't shake the ghosts in the closets of his mind. At five-foot-ten and a rock solid one eighty-five, he's a force of controlled power. He uses his brain more than his brawn, but he won't back down in a brawl, either.

We help him get outside the dive bar we spent the last two hours inside, tossing beer back and playing pool. Outside, the fresh winter air hits him, and he shakes his head.

"It's not that cold," X says, slapping Trapper in the face. "Sober up, sucka."

Trapper smiles as he starts to ready his mind. As drunk as he is, he knows he has to have his head on straight to ride.

"Flank him on either side, but stay behind in case he lays her down. We only have four miles back to the hotel," I order, swinging my leg over my Harley Softail Slim and cranking it. The rumble soothes all that stays wound tight inside me. The vibration reminds me of the power under me.

Blowing out a breath, I tap the gas tank. "Ride for Raleigh," I whisper and point to the night sky. *Never forget*, I remind myself before I move to ride. My hands on the bars, twisting the throttle, I let the bike move me and lift my feet to rest on the pegs. As each of my brother's mount, I pull out, knowing they will hit the throttle and catch me, so I relax as the road passes under me.

We ride as six with no ties to anyone or anything from one city to the next. We have a bond. We are the only family for each other, and we keep it that way. No attachments, no commitments, and that means no casualties.

We are here by choice. Any man can leave the club and our life behind at any time. I trust these men with my life and with my death. When my time is called, they will move on with the missions as they come.

We don't often let one another drink and drive, but coming south, Trapper needed to cut loose for a bit. He may be drunk, yet once the wind hits his face, he will be solid. He always is.

At the no-tell motel we are crashing at, X takes Trapper with him to one of the three shit-ass rooms we booked while Judge and Rowdy go to the other. The place has seen better days, probably thirty years ago. It's a place to shit, shower, and maybe, if I can keep the nightmares away, sleep. I have never needed anything fancy, and tonight is no different.

I give them a half salute as they close their doors and lock down for the night.

Deacon heads on into our room. Always a man of few words and interaction, he doesn't look back or give me any indication that he cares if I follow or stay behind.

I give myself the same moment I take every night and stand out under the stars to smoke.

I look up. Immediately, I can hear her tiny voice in my mind, making up constellations all her own. Raleigh was once a rambunctious little girl. She was afraid of nothing. She loved the night sky and wishing upon all the stars.

Another city, another life, I wish it was another time, but one thing I know is that there is no turning back time. If I could, I would. Not just for me, but for all five of us.

I light my cigarette and take a deep drag. Inhaling, I hold it in my lungs before I blow out. The burn, the taste, and the touch of it to my lips don't ease the thoughts in my mind. Another night is upon us, and it's yet another night Raleigh will never come home.

The receptionist steps out beside me. She isn't the one who was here when we checked in earlier. When she smiles up at me, I can tell she has been waiting on us. Guess the trailer trash from day shift chatted up her replacement. Well, at least this one has nice teeth. Day shift definitely doesn't have dental on her benefit plan here.

"Go back inside," I bark, not really in the mood for company.

"I'm entitled to a break," she challenges with a southern drawl.

"If you want a night with a biker, I'm not the one," I try to warn her off.

"Harley, leather, cigarettes, and sexy—yeah, I think you're the one … for tonight, that is." She comes over and reaches out for the edges of my cut.

I grab her wrists. "You don't touch my cut."

She bites her bottom lip with a sly smile. "Oh, rules. I can play by the rules, big daddy."

I drop her hands and walk in a circle around her before standing in front of her then backing her to the wall. I take another drag of my cigarette and blow the smoke into her face. "I'm not your fucking daddy." I take another long drag. Smoke blows out with each word as I let her know. "If you wanna fuck, we'll fuck. Make no mistake, though, I'm not in the mood to chat, cuddle, or kiss. I'm a man; I'll fuck, and that's it."

She leans her head back, testing me.

"Hands against the wall," I order, and she slaps her palms against the brick behind her loudly.

Her chest rises and falls dramatically as her breathing increases. She keeps licking and biting her lips.

"You want a ride on the wild side?"

She nods, pushing her tits out at me.

"You wet for me?" I ask, and she giggles while nodding. "If you want me to get hard and stay hard, you don't fucking make a sound. That giggling shit is annoying as fuck."

Immediately, she snaps her mouth shut.

I yank her shirt up and pull her bra over her titties without unhooking it. Her nipples point out in the cold night air.

"You cold or is that for me?" I ask, flicking her nipple harshly.

"You," she whispers breathlessly.

I yank the waistband of her stretchy pants down, pulling her panties with them. Her curls glisten with her arousal under the street light.

With her pants at her ankles, I turn her around to face the wall.

"Bend over, grab your ankles. You don't speak, don't touch me, and you don't move. If you want a wild ride with a biker, I'm gonna give you one you'll never forget."

While she positions herself, I grab a condom from my wallet and unbutton my four button jeans enough to release my cock. While stroking myself a few times to get fully erect, part of me considers just walking away. However, I'm a man, and pussy is pussy. No matter what my mood, it's a place to sink into for a time.

Covering myself carefully, I spread her ass cheeks and slide myself inside her slick cunt.

The little whore is more than ready.

I close my eyes and picture a dark-haired beauty with ink covering her arms and a tight cunt made just for me. I can almost hear the gravelly voice of my dream woman as she moans my name, pushing back to take me deeper, thrust after thrust.

I roll my hips as the receptionist struggles to keep herself in position.

Raising my hand, I come down on the exposed globe of her ass cheek. "Dirty fucking girl." I spank her again. "I'm not your fucking daddy, but I'll give you what he obviously didn't." I spank her again and thrust. "Head down between your legs. Watch me fuck your pussy."

She does as instructed and watches as I continue

slamming into her. Stilling, I reach down and twist her nipples as she pushes back on me.

Her moans get louder as I move, gripping her hips and pistoning in and out of her.

I slap her ass again. "I said quiet."

I push deep, my hips hitting her ass, and she shakes as her orgasm overtakes her.

"Fuck me!" she wails.

I slam in and out, in and out, faster and faster, until I explode inside the condom.

She isn't holding her ankles by the time I'm done. She's still head down, bent over with her back against the wall as her hands hang limply like the rest of her body, trembling in aftershocks.

Pulling out, I toss the condom on the ground and walk away, buttoning my pants back up.

"Collector," I hear X yell my road name from his doorway. "You ruined that one." He is smoking a cigarette. It's obvious he watched the show.

The noise has Judge coming to his door and giving me a nod of approval.

I look over my shoulder to see the bitch still hasn't moved. Her pussy is out in the air, ass up, head down, and she's still moaning. Desperate, needy, it's not my thing.

"I need a shower," I say, giving X a two finger

salute before going into my own room. Deacon is already in bed and doesn't move as I go straight back to the shit-ass bathroom to clean up.

I wasn't lying. I smell like a bar, and now I smell the skank stench of easy pussy. I have needs, but I can't help wondering what it would be like to have to work for my release just once. It's not in my cards, though. Just like this town, this ride, and that broad, it's on to the next for me and my brothers of the Devil's Due MC.

Available on all major ebook retailers!

CPSIA information can be obtained
at www.ICGtesting.com
Printed in the USA
LVHW031629080321
680887LV00004B/634

9 781534 718609